Loyalty Is What I Asked For

Amber Meeks

Autumn

"This is why he ain't allowed to drink" I laughed watching my fiancé, Malcolm act a fool in our front yard. Since the pandemic, nobody has been able to really hang out and everybody was getting a little stir crazy. Since it was my man's birthday, I put a little kickback together, inviting all his family and close friends to the house to eat and have some fun. I've seen this man drunk a million times so I knew what to expect, but tonight, he was on a level that I've never seen before. It was funny at first, but he was starting to get on my damn nerves. From pulling his gun out every 5 minutes to stumbling all over the place. I'm not sure if it's because I'm pregnant and can't get on his level, but I'm about ready for him to go sit down somewhere and pass out.

"I'm about to start cleaning up" I told his step mom, Tara, fed up with the sight before me.

"You need some help?" she asked.

"Yeah, you can come help me if you want" I told her and headed in the house to the kitchen. Thankfully, our guests didn't mess up my house as bad as I thought so it was an easy task.

"Aye, sis, come get this nigga. He trippin!" Malcolm's friend Jordan said bursting in the kitchen. I rolled my eyes.

"What do you mean? What happened?"

"This nigga is laid out on the sidewalk drunk as hell with his eyes closed" he said shaking his head.

"Are you serious?" I said trying to hide my irritation by laughing it off.

"Sister, come get your fiancé before I slap the shit out of him!" Shay's voice boomed from behind Jordan.

"I'm coming, Jordan just told me".

"Nah, this nigga is trippin. My nephew is out there crying! He thinks this nigga is dead because he ain't getting up".

The mention of my son crying made my blood boil instantly. This was part of the reason why I didn't want kids here, but all my baby sitters were here so I figured it would be fine.

I raced out the house and to the front yard, instantly noticing the small crowd of people in a circle. I quickly found my son and sure enough, he had a face full of tears. When he noticed me he ran up to me and I embraced him.

"It's ok baby!" I said hugging him and stroking his head.

"What's wrong with my Daddy?" he cried. I looked over at Malcolm laid out on the ground with a slight smile on his face and rolled my eyes.

"Nothing is wrong. Daddy is just acting silly. He's fine, I promise. Go with TT and go get in the bed, ok?" I said glancing up at Shay. He nodded his head and walked off with his aunt. Once he was out of sight, I marched over to Malcolm and hovered over him. I observed his big goofy ass frame. Even though I was pissed, his drunk ass was still fine. Almond shaped brown eyes, a full beard, big ass soup cooler lips, caramel skin and a baller belly. Still, even with all that fineness, he had me fucked up in this moment. Wasting no time, I began to land blow after blow to his chest.

"Get yo stupid ass up! Your son was just crying because he thinks you're dead!"

"Aye! Aye! Aye! You ain't gotta beat his ass like that!" I heard somebody yell but I didn't give a fuck. It was one thing to be drunk, but to be that fucked up to the point your child thinks you're dead, is where I draw the line. Plus, we were on my property, I can do what the fuck I want to do and nobody can stop me.

"I don't give a fuck! Get yo ass up!" I said slightly kicking him. That seemed to get his attention because he quickly sat up.

"Come on bro. You in trouble" Malcolm's friend Terrell teased. A couple of his other friends helped his big ass up.

"Bae, you mad at me?" he asked, slurring his words.

"Don't say shit to me" I snarled.

I watched as his friends picked him up and drug him from the sidewalk in front of the house all the way to the side door. After struggling to get him in the door, he fell in the hallway.

"I know you don't think you're about to just leave him right here and leave me to drag him up the stairs by myself?" I asked his friends pointing to the staircase.

"Man, sis, leave that nigga right here. He'll be alright".

"Absolutely not! Just so my baby can wake up in the morning and think his Daddy died again? No! Get him upstairs". We stared at each other for a moment. When they realized that I wasn't going to back down, they did as I requested.

"I ain't tryna go upstairs! I'm good right here. Just give me a minute, Imma get up and go myself" Malcolm said barely above a whisper.

"See". I cut my eyes at Terrell. He put his hands up in surrender.

"You gotta know that I don't give a fuck about what he talking about. Get him upstairs". Again, we stared at each other for a few moments before they reluctantly drug his big ass up the steps and into our bedroom. Once they got him in the room, I began to undress him as best as I could. I grabbed the trash can, placed it at the side of the bed, tucked him in like a big ass baby and just looked at him. Although he pissed me off tonight, I know he enjoyed his self and will probably regret drinking so much in the morning.

"Autumn, are you coming back down?" Shay yelled from

downstairs.

"Yeah, here I come!" I yelled back.

I straightened up a few more things in the room and just as I was about to walk out, I heard Malcolm's phone going off. *I should probably put it on the charger,* I thought. Walking towards the ringing, I grabbed his pants that were on the floor and dug through his pocket until I retrieved the phone. I glanced at the missed notification and instantly froze. I recognized this number.

Gripping the phone in my hand, I glanced at Malcolm then back at the phone. Part of me wanted to just put the phone on the charger and walk away, but the other half said fuck that, find out what's going on. I connected the phone to the charger and unlocked his phone. Immediately, I went to his messages and of course, the number was the first one to appear. I tapped on the thread and started scrolling up. With each second that passed by, my anger grew. I didn't bother to read every single message because I knew what it was just from skimming. I went back to the last message that was sent and saw that it was a picture he sent her of him in front of her house saying *I'm outside*. I looked at the time and date and saw that this shit was yesterday afternoon. Not only that, but he had the audacity to be in my car at the time. *This nigga got me so fucked up.*

I wanted to cry, but not out of sadness, more so out of anger. This shit felt like déjà vu and it's part of the reason why I was so reluctant to do this again. Five years ago, when our son MJ was first born, I found out that Malcolm was cheating on me with this girl named Kimora. They fucked around for months before I found out, which means he cheated while I was pregnant. I was crushed to say the least.

My pregnancy was rough, especially since it was my first child. We were in such a dark place back then. We argued all the time over his cheating. I went through post-partum and dealt with a heartbreak all at the same time, but still, I wanted to make it work. Not just for MJ, but because I truly loved him and felt like

I deserved to have him. We went back and forth for three or four years and finally, I felt like he got his shit together. He stuck by me and was there for me when my best friend passed away. He showed me a side of him that I've never seen, proposed and really had me thinking that shit was different. So much so, that here I am 8 months pregnant with our second child and just that quick, it's like all that progress meant nothing.

I was hurt, but I couldn't bring myself to shed any tears about this. Instead, I screenshot messages and call logs, sent them to my email and deleted the evidence of the screenshots from his phone. I knew exactly how to handle this.

***

A few days passed since his birthday, and I still hadn't brought up the messages. I let him walk around thinking shit was sweet, just waiting for the right moment. I observed the way he behaved and finally noticed a few red flags that I hadn't before. I came down to the den where he played his game. I rarely ever sat in the den but I noticed that he would quickly put his phone down or slightly jump like I caught him off guard, but I pretended that I didn't' see it.

"What's wrong with you?" Malcolm asked laying down next to me in our bed.

"Nothing, why do you say that?" I asked looking at him in his eyes. Flashes of all our history played like a movie in my mind. There was a time I was so in love with this man. He could do no wrong to me. Even now, looking at those almond shaped brown eyes and those big ass lips, he was still handsome, but he was also a piece of shit, and I knew it.

"Stop playing Autumn, I know when you aren't really yourself, so talk to me". *He wants to do this right now? No problem,* I thought. I sat up straight in the bed and looked at him.

"*Okay*...I just have one question for you and please don't insult my intelligence and lie to me" I stated.

"Okay".

"How long have you been back talking to Kimora?" I asked in a calm even tone.

"What do you mean?" he asked, playing dumb.

"Malcolm, I'll smack the shit out of you" I said calmly.

"It wasn't shit like that for real. She was telling me happy birthday and catching up, nothing major".

"So, you haven't seen her or tried to see her?"

"Nah" he said lying straight to my face.

"You haven't?"

"I just said no" he said getting a little defensive.

Normally, that shit would make me mad, but instead, it just confirmed what I was already feeling. Instead of responding, I reached over and grabbed my phone off the night stand. Unlocking it, I tapped the screen a few times until I found what I was looking for and shoved the phone in his face. I watched as he tried to focus on the phone, waiting for any slight change in his facial expression. He grabbed the phone and stared at it for a few seconds and then looked at me.

"That's crrazy how you just lied in my face, ain't it?"

"Autumn..look" he started to say. I held my hand up to stop him.

"Honestly, I don't even wanna hear it. I already know what you're about to say Malcolm. You say the same shit every single time you get caught and at this point, it's very tired. I'm just upset that I really thought you changed. I really thought we were past all of this. When we first found out I was pregnant, I told yo ass that I was afraid this would happen. You used to say how you don't know how to handle my emotions or deal with me while I'm pregnant and I believed you. I told you exactly how I felt about that situation and still you decided to do the same thing with the same girl! Like damn! You think that makes me feel good?! I'm so over this shit!" I yelled. I could feel my blood boiling and tears forming. All I could think about is getting as far away from him as possible.

I quickly hopped out of the bed, put on my Nike slides and walked out of the room and down the steps. Per usual, Malcolm was right behind me trying to talk to me and convince me that what it's "not like that". If I had $1 for every time that I've heard that line from him, I'd be able to buy a new car.

"Autumn chill the fuck out! I'm not trying argue with you".

"Just leave me alone man. Like for real".

"Nah, tell me wassup".

"What do you mean?"

"What are you trying do?"

"What do you mean what am I trying to do? I'm not trying to do shit. I'm over this shit and I'm over you. I'm not going through this shit again with you". He stared at me for a second, trying to gauge if I was serious or not and then nodded his head.

"Bet" he said and walked away.

Rolling my eyes, I walked out of the house and got in my car. I didn't have anywhere to go and I didn't want to put anybody in the middle of me and Malcolm's bullshit. So instead of pulling off, I just sat there with my thoughts. I told myself I'd never let this shit happen to me again and I meant that shit. Ten damn years down the drain all because this nigga can never act right, but it's okay, because I can show him better than I can tell him.

Malcolm

I've never been more confused about Autumn and I's relationship than I am right now. Ever since the day she caught my ass talking to Kimora, she's been different. She's not really fucking with me, but sometimes she acts like everything is fine. For example, we had our baby shower a few weeks ago and she acted like everything was just fine and she was so happy. Everybody had a great time, including myself. I wanted to ask her what we were doing because she was sending mixed signals, but I really wasn't trying to argue with her ass. All that damn yelling, screaming and crying, I can't take it.

I wish she understood that sometimes I need somebody else to talk to because I can't talk to her about anything. I can't tell her that though, because she never thinks she does anything wrong. I swear, if you tell this girl she's wrong, all hell will break loose. Kimora is just cool people. I'd be lying if I said I didn't wanna hit again, but I really wasn't on that for the most part. Once again, I can't tell Autumn's ass because she's gonna believe whatever she wants. I'm so ready for her to drop this baby so we can get shit back on track. It's something about a woman when she's pregnant. She was already emotional as hell, but pregnancy takes it to a whole new level that I just can't deal with. Sometimes I just wanna strangle her ass so she can chill the fuck out.

"Aye, I can't hold it in no more. I need to know wassup" I blurted out. She looked over at me with a frown.

"What are you talking about?" she asked.

"This" I said waving my finger between me and her. "What

is this? Are we together or not?”

“Why are you asking me that? You tryna justify all that bullshit you be on?” I let out a frustrated breath before responding.

“I’m just asking so I know how to move Autumn”.

“I don’t know” she said lowly.

“What do you mean you don’t know? It’s a yes or no question”.

“It’s not that easy”.

“How isn’t it? You either wanna be with me or you don’t. You’re only thinking about it from your point of view, you ain’t thinking about how us really breaking up would affect me”.

“Boy fuck you! All the shit you’ve done to me?! All the hurt…physically, mentally, emotionally and you’re talking about how us breaking up would affect you!? Are you dumb?” she yelled.

“Bro, listen, if we break up, and I mean really break up, you’ll be good regardless. I’m the one that gotta worry about where the fuck I’m about to live and all that extra shit. You ain’t got shit to worry about”.

“Maybe you should’ve thought about that before you were out here doing your pregnant fiancé dirty. Ask Kimora can you live with her”. That stung, but I shrugged it off.

“So, you’re saying we done right?”

“Done as fuck” she said matter of factly.

“Alright, so how long do I have to move out?”

“I don’t know right now; we can figure that out later” she said trying to walk out of the room. I quickly stood in front of the door.

“Malcolm, move!” she yelled.

“No. You always wanna try and run away from shit. Stop acting like a fucking little kid all the time” I said getting irritated with this conversation. I really wasn’t trying to argue with her, I just wanted to make things clear and come to an understanding.

"A little kid?! I'm a little kid!? Nigga are you serious? You're the one who can't even be a mature enough man to deal with a woman you claim to love while she's carrying YOUR child. Talking about you don't know how to handle my emotions. That's some weak ass shit. I'm acting like a little kid because I'm trying get the fuck away from you? I don't wanna continue with this conversation and I don't have to if I don't want to. So, like I said, move out of my way" she yelled trying to push me out of the way.

"Man, watch out" I said gently pushing her.

"Don't fucking touch me!"

"I swear to God I'm not doing this shit with you bro. Chill yo ass the fuck out and talk like you got some sense. I understand you mad, hurt and all that but you need to relax".

"I ain't gotta relax shit! I'm so fucking tired of you! You always want somebody to calm down after you did some shit to them. I'm really starting to hate you bro. You always wanna justify why you do certain shit and then try to act nonchalant like you don't give a fuck". She looked so hurt, and I hate that I was the reason for the hurt, but I'm tired of having this same fucking argument. She loved acting like she was the victim, like I can't do shit right. What man wants to keep hearing that shit?

"I'm starting not to give a fuck. You make it seem like I can't do shit right" I stated honestly.

"You can't! Every time I think you've changed, you prove me wrong. I feel so fucking stupid for staying with you man" she said looking defeated. Instead of trying to get out, she went to the other side of the room. I palmed my face.

"I wish you would shut the fuck up bro. I'm so tired of hearing this shit. You just perfect huh? You don't do shit, right!? Autumn is just a fucking angel!" I yelled.

"What have I done to you that was so bad?!" she screamed.

"You don't fucking get it! You think just because you ain't out here cheating that you're walking around this bitch perfect!? You ain't perfect Autumn! You think I wanna be out here talking to another female? I don't! But I can't talk to yo ass because this is what I get!" I yelled.

"You never tried! You've never tried to talk to me. You've never come to me and put shit on the table telling me how you really feel. You never say shit until you get caught doing some shit and now it sounds like you're pulling excuses out ya ass! I don't wanna hear that shit man. I'm so done with you, bro I swear!" she screamed getting off the bed. Without thinking, I reached in the closet, grabbed my strap, and pointed it at her

"Done with who? Where the fuck you think you going, huh? Sit the fuck down!" I yelled in a rage, waving the gun at her. I watched as Autumn's eyes got big and nothing but fear consumed her. She put her hands up and screamed.

"Malcolm, stop! Are you fucking crazy!? I'm pregnant!!"

"I don't give a fuck! You keep making it seem like I'm the bad guy. Always wanna put Malcolm in the wrong. Talk that shit now! Huh? I don't fucking hear you!" I screamed in rage.

"Ok! Ok! I'm sorry! Please!" she begged and screamed. I stared at her. Finally, I realized that I was pointing a gun at my pregnant fiancé. Regret washed over me. I felt like shit looking at the horrified expression on her face, covered with tears. *Damn,* I thought to myself. I wanted to say something, but what could I say after that shit?

I stood frozen in place, watching her regain her composure and all but run out of the room and down the steps. A few moments later, I heard the door slam, jolting me out of my frozen state.

"FUCK!"

Durell

"Aye brody, you don't hear me talking to you?" Isaiah asked.

"Hell nah, wassup?" I responded shaking my head trying to get rid of my thoughts.

"Nothing now. What the fuck is wrong with you?"

"Shit. I'm good bro. Let's go" I said starting my car up and pulling off. We were headed to work, but my mind was all over the place. I hated telling this nigga shit because I felt like he pillow talked with the hoes he fucked around with and I don't have time for no extra mothafuckas in my business. Granted, he was my brother and blood couldn't make us any closer, but there were certain people that you had to handle a certain way.

We vibed to the music blasting through my speakers as I eased my way through the city traffic. I was ready to get this shift over with already. This working shit really wasn't for me. I was used to being in the streets, but I was trying to change for the better. If I was being honest, I'm getting too old for all that street shit anyway. Plus, I got kids that need me and if I continued doing what I was doing, I wouldn't be around to see them grow up and I couldn't have that.

Thankfully, my work shift went by quickly. All I wanted to do was grab something to eat, smoke and go to sleep, but as soon as I pulled in the driveway, I knew God had other plans for me. I let out a frustrated breath before climbing out of the car and going inside the house.

"Dang, you ain't bring me no food?" she asked as soon as I stepped foot in the house.

"My bad, I thought you would be sleep" I responded. She smacked her lips.

"You're selfish as fuck. You know I'm not sleep around this time".

"Man, please don't start with me. I just wanna eat, smoke and go to sleep. Can I do that?"

"You can do whatever you want to do my baby" she said and walked off with an attitude. Letting out a frustrated sigh I shook my head and sat on the couch ready to devour my food.

"Where's the boys?" I asked noticing that the house was unusually quiet.

"In their room, sleep. Where else would they be?" she snapped. I leaned my head back and closed my eyes. *Every damn day she got an attitude. I ain't even did shit.*

Rochelle is my on again/off again girlfriend and the mother of my two youngest sons. She was an average looking light skin girl with a decent body, but the pussy and head was fire, I had to give it to her. They weren't lying when they said the best pussy is attached to a crazy bitch because she was definitely out her shit; but she'd been there through a lot of my bullshit and loved me, so I fucked with her heavy. Shit, I even loved her, I mean, how could I not after all the shit we been through.

I met her about five years ago. I was going through it, in and out of jail, in the street shit and she was like a breath of fresh air. I fucked with her vibe. We did everything together for real, shopping, a couple trips, turning up. After a while, shit started to go sour. Her attitude changed from sugar to shit very quickly. She started accusing me of cheating (when I wasn't) and would pop off at the slightest inconvenience.

I know she dealt with a lot in her past, with cheating and abuse, but I wasn't that nigga. At least, I tried not to be. I hated doing all that arguing, so I felt like, if you're going to accuse me anyway, I might as well do what you're accusing me of. That's when the on again, off again shit started.

She'd go through my phone and catch me talking to a girl, argue with me, her or any fucking body and then we'd be back together. There was one girl that I was fucking with heavy who ended up pregnant. We weren't together at the time that this happened, but Rocehlle didn't care. The girl ended up having a miscarriage, and even though I felt bad, I was kind of relieved. I had enough kids. After the miscarriage, Rochelle harrassed the girl, going back and forth on the internet. That was one thing that I hated about her ass. Why are you confronting every girl you think I have interest in? Especially when we aren't together.

Right now, we weren't together at the moment, but of course we still fucked from time to time and I still had a key so I came and went as I pleased. We had an understanding.

After I ate and smoked, I realized she hadn't come back in the living room which meant she went to bed and I didn't have to hear shit else come out of her smart-ass mouth. Pulling my phone out of my pocket, I checked my texts and then scrolled through social media, stopping once a particular picture caught my eye. *Look at my dog. Her fine ass looks happy. I'm happy for her, she deserves it,* I thought to myself. I stared at the picture for a few more minutes, debating if I should reach out and catch up or just leave her alone. Just as I was about to send her a message, a text from Rochelle popped up at the top of my screen.

BM: Come here

Already knowing what that meant, I happily got my ass up and went to satisfy her.

Autumn

I'd been staying in a hotel with MJ the last few days, but I needed to take my ass back home. Malcolm has been blowing my phone up of course. We did talk when I first got here and I let him know where I was. He tried to plead his case by saying "I wasn't really going to shoot you, I Just wanted you to chill out". That right there did it for me. He continued to call my phone and I let him talk to MJ, but other than that, I didn't have shit to say to him. I've never been more terrified of a human being than I was that night. I still can't believe that shit happened to me.

I really didn't even want to go back to the house with him there, but I didn't have a choice. I can't keep paying for this hotel while he's chilling in my house with no worries. I had some time to think, and I knew that I'd have to go home and have a hard conversation with him. I really didn't want it to turn into another argument out of fear that I'd go into labor early, but I had to do what I had to do.

Pulling up to the house, I took a deep breath. I was grateful that MJ was at daycare right now so I didn't have to worry about him hearing or seeing anything that he shouldn't be exposed to. He's had enough of that and I hate that I ever allowed it to get this far.

"Malcolm!" I called out as soon as I stepped foot through the front door. Seconds later, he appeared coming down the steps.

"Are you ok?" he asked. I nodded my head yes.

"I wanna talk to you. But I want to actually talk. I don't want to argue". He stared at me for a second, took a deep breath and then nodded his head. I went to the couch in the living room and took a seat. He sat down next to me and I scooted away slightly. There was a hint of irritation on his face when I moved away but it was quickly replaced with his normal mug.

"What do you wanna talk about Autumn?"

"Us. I think it's time that we actually address the elephant in the room, make intentions clear and figure out what we're going to do".

"Meaning what? You don't wanna be together anymore?"

"No, I don't. Can you honestly say that you're happy with me Malcolm? Like, look me in my eyes and say you're happy".

"I am. I swear I am. I only want to be with you".

"How when you keep cheating?" he let out a frustrated sigh, running his hand down his face.

"Man, I don't know how many times I have to tell you I haven't cheated on you. Was I talking to her? Yeah. Did I pull up on her? Yeah. But we haven't went out, fucked, nothing! She knows you're pregnant and all. It's really not like that between us. I just wish you knew like I knew".

"You keep saying that but you never want to take into account how I feel. You.."

"I do though! You just think I don't. I understand how you feel".

"You couldn't possibly understand...or maybe you do and just don't give a fuck, because there's no way that you still do what you want to do knowing how it will make me feel. That makes me feel like you don't really give a fuck about me because I'd never do anything that I know would hurt you. You don't be thinking about me, you only think about yourself and I can't deal with that shit anymore". I made sure to look him in his eyes so that he knew I was dead ass serious. I kept my tone of voice calm and collected but stern. I couldn't act like it wasn't hurting me to say this, but it needed to be said and done.

"I mean, it's obvious that I can't change your mind, so I'll just have to deal with your choice. I'm not gonna do too much talking, Imma just show you" he said. It felt like a bunch of bullshit, so I wasn't going to respond to his statement. "How is this about to work with us living together but not together?" I gave him a blank stare.

"What do you mean how is it going to work? You're going to have to move. I'm going to be fair since your name is on the lease, but once the lease is up which is at the end of the year, you gotta go. Not trying to sound harsh, but it is what it is" I told him. Instead of responding, he nodded his head, got up and walked away. I didn't expect this to go so well, but I'm glad it had. I was tired of fighting with this man about everything.

A part of me wanted him to be serious about showing me rather than telling me that he would change. I wanted to believe him, I really did, but I thought he had changed this time around. He was doing so good honestly. Of course, we had our arguments here and there as any couple does, but I really thought he was done with the cheating and it hurts to know that every time I'm carrying this man's baby he chooses to step out on me. Like damn. Am I that hard to deal with when I'm pregnant?

Malcolm

"Damn, so y'all really done?" my nigga T asked. We were sitting at his house chilling and drinking. Shit at home was rough and I was uncomfortable as fuck. I didn't really want to be around her knowing how she felt about me, and I know a lot of that was my fault, but what the fuck can I do about that shit now? She's going to always hold a grudge and look at me the way she does.

I realize because of our history, she feels a certain way, especially when we get into it. I'm not saying that I'm perfect, but shit I really tried with her ass. I even got down on one knee and asked her to marry me. That shit was real. I meant it and I thought we had worked past our shit but obviously not.

Shit with me and Kimora really wasn't on what Autumn thought it was. I wasn't lying when I said she was just my dog. I mean, did I wanna fuck her one more time, hell yeah. I'm a man, I'd be lying if I said I didn't. She was thick as hell. Shit, thicker than Autumn, and that's saying a lot.

I couldn't act like my girl wasn't cold. That brown skin, big eyes, perfect lips, thick thighs and a fat ass. Not to mention, she had a great personality, super understanding and all around had a lot going for herself. Obviously, she had a little gut, but that came from carrying my Junior, and now she had another one that I'd get to meet in the morning. She had a C-Section scheduled for tomorrow morning and for some reason, I was a little nervous.

"Yeah, I think we really are done. I mean, since we had that talk a couple of weeks ago, she's been cool, we haven't had any problems, but it literally feels like we're just roommates that sleep in the same bed. It's weird as fuck. And I ain't getting no pussy! I might as well have been cheating for real, at least I'd be getting some!" T laughed, shaking his head.

"Nigga, you a piece of shit".

"I'm dead ass. Shit, I could've made it worth it. Now I gotta find a place to live, worry about getting furniture and all that. Only thing I can say, she told me the other day that she only wants me to help her with half the rent, other than that, she told me to just focus on stacking so I can move".

"Aye, I ain't gon lie sis the goat for that one. You better appreciate that shit, a lot of these females would've been like nigga you still got responsibilities so you better figure it out" he said mocking the way females talk. I chuckled.

"You stupid, but you right" I responded taking a sip of my drink. I expected to feel a burning sensation go down my throat, but I felt nothing. Instead, the liquor tasted like water. That was my sign to stop drinking. "This my last drink. If I get too fucked up and spend the night over here Autumn will kill me".

"My nigga about be a father of two in the morning. That shit is crazy".

"It ain't that crazy. I been with her for damn near ten years. It was bound to happen".

"Yeah, but I thought y'all would be one and done the way sis was so adamant about not having any more kids".

"Lowkey, I thought the same. When she told me she was pregnant with Armon, I thought she was going to get an abortion. I'm happy she didn't though" I said reflecting on the last ten months.

"Me too. I can't wait to meet lil neph. And you'll be alright fool, you always land on your feet" he said dapping me up and pulling me in for a quick hug.

***

"You ready?" I asked Autumn, looking around the room making sure we got everything.

"Yeah I'm ready" she said getting off the bed and putting her slides on.

I couldn't help but admire her in this moment. Here she was, about to give birth to our second child and she was looking like it wasn't shit to her. She was dressed comfortably in a pair of yoga shorts and a t-shirt but she looked amazing. Her hair and nails were done and she made sure to do her eyebrows and put on some lashes. I asked her why she was doing all of that just to be sitting in the hospital and she said she had to be cute when she gave birth so nobody would be talking about her when they saw the pictures. I just laughed and shook my head because why is that what you're worried about? Female shit.

When we got to the hospital, they checked her in and then took her to a "waiting room" and hooked up IV's and some other shit to her to monitor her and the baby. They came in to check on her a few times and kept assuring us that the doctor would be ready soon. I was bored as hell just sitting there waiting in that cold ass hospital, so I eventually fell asleep.

"Everything looks good. We're going to prep you to go into an OR in about fifteen minutes. Your doctor will be there to talk to you, ok?" I heard the nurse say. Autumn agreed.

"You ready?" I asked, waking up. She looked over at me and gave me a small smile.

"How many times are you gonna ask me that?" she chuckled.

"Shit, my bad. I'm just making sure you're good".

"I'm good. I'm really just ready for him to be here. I wanna hold him. I'm also tired of being uncomfortable. So yeah, I'm ready as hell" she said and I nodded.

Finally, the nurse came and got her to take her to the operating room. I couldn't go back with her until they were ready to do the C-Section. I didn't really like that shit, but I couldn't do anything about it. After about fifteen more minutes of waiting someone came and got me to take me back and had me put on a gown, a hair net and some other shit before going in.

When I got there, I saw a hand full of people moving around the room quickly, talking amongst themselves about the procedure. The lady that came to get me led me to Autumn, and for a second, I froze. She was laying there with her eyes closed, not moving.

"Aye, is she ok!?" I all but shouted. A few people standing close to me jumped slightly at the sound of my voice. The male doctor that was the closest to her looked up at me and slightly smiled the way white people smile at niggas.

"Hi. I'm assuming you're Dad. I'm the anesthesiologist. We just gave her some medicine to numb her, but I can assure you she's ok". His tone was even and comforting, but Autumn still hadn't opened her eyes, even with me raising my voice. I walked over to her and touched her shoulder.

"Autumn?"

"I'm ok. I hear you being a crazy person" she said smiling lazily. I could tell that whatever medicine they gave her was kicking in. Home girl was lit. I sat in the chair next to her and looked around the room. I hated hospitals ever since my mom passed away. I was sixteen when she passed and I did my best to avoid the hospital at all cost.

Autumn's doctor walked in, congratulated us and spoke to everyone else in the room while getting prepped.

"Ok, we're about to start the procedure. I just ask that you stay seated and do not look over the barrier that we have in place. We don't want you to be creeped out" Autumn's doctor said to me. I nodded my head. I remember when MJ was born. I wasn't there, but I heard the story from Autumn's Mom about how she looked over the barrier even though they told her not to. She said she saw all Autumn's insides and was grossed out. They didn't have to worry about me. I wouldn't dare get my black ass up to look at that shit. I'll pass the fuck out and all three of would be admitted in this bitch.

"It should only take about 30-45 minutes. Once the baby is delivered, we'll clean him up, get his vitals and everything and then I'll hand him over to you. You'll be able to take pictures and do whatever once they get him over to clean him up. We'll close Autumn up and then take both her and the baby to recovery and you can follow us there and sit with them. Sound good?" she asked. I nodded and looked over at Autumn. She smiled and then looked up at the ceiling.

The procedure seemed like it was taking forever as I watched the doctor tugging and pulling at Autumn's midsection. I was about to fall asleep until I heard someone say "there he is!". My eyes shot open and I hopped up, but then quickly sat back down remembering that Autumn's insides were currently outside of her body.

"Did you see him?"

"Hell nah, I remembered your insides was out so I sat my stupid ass back down" I said joining her in a chuckle.

"We really have two kids now. That's crazy" she said smiling lazily.

"Hell yeah it is. You didn't feel none of that shit?"

"Nope. Not at all. This was way smoother than MJ. I felt a lot of it, and I was so cold I was in there shivering and throwing up" she said. Her eyes saddened for a split second while she reminisced on the birth of our first born, but she quickly shifted her eyes to the left of me. I followed her gaze and landed on the nurses cleaning off my boy.

"I'm gonna go take some pictures for you" I told her getting up and going over to see him for the first time.

As I got closer, I smiled. I don't get why babies always come out white, but I could tell this was my kid. He looked a lot like MJ when he was first born, but I could see Autumn in him too. Getting a closer look at him, I was proud. My baby boy. I let them clean him up and get him wrapped up and then they handed him to me. Being the first one to hold him in my arms was hands down the best feeling, but I also felt a little guilty. Guilty due to the fact that I know I stressed his mom out the last part of her pregnancy. I glanced at Autumn who was staring at us, waiting for me to bring her baby to her. I wanted to change for her, but I felt like it was way too late, so I might as well keep doing what I'm doing.

Autumn

Today was a day that I never thought would come...Malcolm moving out. Since having Armon, we've found a way to co-exist as friends and as parents. Well, it took a while to get here. The first couple of months after Armon was born was rough. He played nice for a couple of weeks and I got comfortable, falling back into the same routine. We argued about Kimora, and the boy literally spit in my face while I had Armon in my arms. That right there was my final straw. I attempted to call the police and put him out, but since his name was on the lease and he'd been staying there for more than 60 days, they couldn't just kick him out. We had no choice but to make it work for the time being. Now, we were able to co-exist and be co-parents building towards a friendship.

I felt good about my decision to end things with him. So much so, that I offered to help him get a few household items. I'd been doing great with keeping up with the bills and everyone's upkeep on my own so I had some extra to give. It sounds crazy when explaining it to other people, but I didn't really care. I didn't want my kids (mainly MJ) to feel like they were missing anything at Daddy's house. My Mom says it should be his responsibility since he's a grown ass man, but me being me, I was going to help him even when I probably shouldn't.

"This is nice" I complimented looking around the apartment. He moved about 10 minutes away from us and about two minutes away from my mom which worked perfectly for me.

"Thanks. It's just enough space for me and the boys when

they're here" he said and I nodded in agreement. He'd asked if I'd be able to drive him around to pick some things up since I had the larger vehicle and I agreed.

I'd been at his house for a few hours, and I noticed Armon getting sleepy, so I decided to head out. I watched as Malcolm kissed the kids and assisted me with getting them in the car. As I climbed in the driver's seat and started up the car, I watched him walk toward the front door of his complex. It felt weird, but in a good way. This chapter of our lives closing for good. We were officially done, living separately and just co-parenting. I could only pray that it stayed peaceful like this.

***

3 months later...

Shit had been going smooth since Malcolm moved. I could honestly say that I was happy. There was no drama in my life, I had a great job that allowed me to work from home and be with my kids making good money, my kids were happy and healthy, my side hustle as a fiction author was going quite well and I'm still a bad bitch. Life couldn't get any better. Well, it could. I could meet the love of my life and live happily ever after, but I needed to be single for a while. Especially since this trip to Miami with my girls is coming up. I planned on being fine and drunk the entire time.

"You don't hear me talking to you, crazy girl?" Malcolm said snapping me out of my thoughts.

"Damn my bad, I didn't even realize y'all came outside" I said unlocking the door to allow Malcolm to put the kids in the car. "What did you say?"

"I said my schedule is about to change soon, so our days are gonna have to change".

"That's cool, just let me know" I told him.

Although, I'd like it if we did one week on and one week off with the kids, for now Malcolm got them on his off days and I had them the rest of the week. I wasn't complaining, but I know that the boys, especially MJ is used to having his Daddy around every day. He hasn't said anything about it, and I've even asked him, so I guess for now it's fine. I looked up and just as I was about to pull off, I saw a little girl standing in the window of Malcolm's apartment. I frowned.

"Did you have fun at your Daddy's house baby?"

"Yeah, Daddy friend was over there with her daughter" he said. I glanced in my rearview mirror and looked at him.

"Oh, Daddy had a friend over? Is her daughter nice?"

"Yeah, but she's a little weird". I chuckled.

"Why is she weird?"

"I don't know. She just kept following me".

"Were you nice to her?"

"Yes, and I shared when we were playing Daddy game".

"Ok good. Where was your brother when you and her were playing Daddy's game?"

"Everybody was in Daddy's room".

"Oh ok" I said and continued driving.

If it was one thing about it, my baby was going to spill the tea. I didn't mind that Malcolm had company, but it bothered me that he didn't bother to let me know or even ask if I was comfortable having my kids around some random girl and her kid. I was going to talk to him about it, but I wanted to see if he would bring it up first. Knowing him, he wouldn't.

Durrell

"If you don't get the fuck out of my face! You sound dumb as hell" I shouted at Rochelle. Here we were having the same argument for the 1,000th time.

"I sound dumb, but you're here damn near every fucking day, fucking on me and acting like we're a family and shit, but then scream we not together. If we're not together then let's not be together then. That shit is confusing as fuck. You just don't want me fucking with nobody else, but you can do whatever" she yelled angrily.

"Girl, I don't give a fuck what you do or who you do it with. I promise you that. You don't want me here, I don't have a problem leaving. You act like I don't have my own shit!"

"Get the fuck out Durrell!" she said pushing me towards the door. As bad as I wanted to respond, I decided not to. It wasn't even worth it. Plus, I had better shit to do than sit there and argue with her. Shit, she wasn't even my girl, doing all that extra shit.

"You need to stop fucking her, that would solve all your problems with her crazy ass" my nigga Isaiah said as soon as I hopped in the whip.

"Shut the fuck up" I snapped, starting the engine and pulling off.

"I'm just saying. I keep tryna tell yo ass. If you don't wanna be with the girl, don't be with her in no kind of way! But, I can't tell you what to do with ya dick. Plus, I know how that baby mama pussy be" he said and I laughed.

"You dumb as fuck". We continued to drive heading downtown to drink, smoke and enjoy the weather.

"Damn I'm proud of sis" Isaiah said. I glanced over to see him looking at his phone.

"Who you talkin' about bro?"

"Autumn" he said. I almost crashed the car just hearing her name. "Damn nigga!" he shouted as I jerked the car back into my lane.

"My bad. What did she do though?" I asked, completely interested in whatever he was about to say.

"She's having a sale on her books. I didn't know she wrote so many" he said and I smiled slightly.

"For real?" I asked tryna play it off like I didn't really care. He said yeah and then changed the subject talking about some bullshit. Once we made it to our destination, we parked and he started rolling up so we could smoke. I took that time to pull my phone out and go to Facebook. As if the universe knew what I opened the app for, Autumn's post was the first thing I saw. *$5 book sale, EVERYTHING MUST GO, DM me if you're interested!* I noticed that she was currently online, so without thinking twice, I opened the messenger app and slid in her DM.

Me: I want a book

Almost instantly, she responded.

*Autumn: Nigga you don't even read *laughing emoji**

*Me: *laughing emoji* I'm tryna support you!*

Autumn: Lol. Where you at?

Me: Downtown

Autumn: You coming to me or I'm coming to you?

Me: Imma be here for a while, pull up

Autumn: Ok, I got a couple drop offs to do, I'll let you know when I'm on my way

Me: Bet

Autumn is one of my oldest female friends, but she holds a special place in a nigga's heart. She was my first girlfriend, my first love and the first girl to introduce me to sex (she took a nigga's virginity). We broke up way back when she was 16 and I was 15. I don't think either one of us expected to be together forever back then. We were just young and in love, or what our young asses thought was love.

She loves to say that I "had a baby on her", but by the time I got my first baby mama pregnant, we were already broken up. Still fucking around, but broken up. She ain't trying to hear that though, even til this day. I bet if I bring it up when she pulls up, she'll get mad as hell. I chuckled to myself. That girl was something different, but in a good way. Plus, it didn't hurt that we were the same zodiac sign, so we understood each other in ways that a lot of people didn't.

"Bitch you over there day dreaming and shit" Isaiah said laughing. I looked at him and then looked behind me. I didn't even realize that a couple of my other homeboys had pulled up and were sitting in the car with us. They definitely caught me slippin.

"Fuck you. Wassup gang" I said greeting the two in the back. They greeted me back with a head nod.

"The fuck was you over there thinking about? Chelle's ass?" Isaiah's nosy ass asked. Before I could respond, my phone rang. I looked down at the screen and saw Autumn's name appear.

"What's the deal!" I answered.

"You still downtown?" she asked. I couldn't help but smile. She still had the cutest voice to me, sounding all innocent.

"Yeah, you pulling up?"

"Yeah, where exactly are you?"

"We at the riverwalk in the parking lot".

"Alright, I'll be there in like 15 minutes".

"Who bouta pull up?" Isaiah's nosy ass asked.

"Damn nigga you all in my business".

"I can't help it mothafucka, you right here".

I never answered his question. We continued to go back and forth and somehow managed to smoke a couple more woods. Again, my phone rang.

"You here?"

"Yeah".

"I'm in this black Chrysler at the front where you walk in at" I told her.

"Oh, I see you. Ok" she said and disconnected the line.

A few moments later, a blue truck pulled up on the side of us and stopped. I looked over and there her fine ass was. I haven't seen this girl in years, but we kept in touch here and there throughout the years. She always seemed to be there when I really needed somebody to talk to about relationship shit and vice versa. She was always down to listen or give advice.

She fumbled around with something in her passenger seat and then looked up. When she noticed me, she smiled. I smiled back.

"Oh shit, that's sis!" Isaiah said and quickly hopped out the car. "What up sis!" he said making his way to her driver's side door.

"Hey brother!" she said excitedly.

"What the fuck you doing here?"

"Yo friend said he wanted some books from me" she said. I opened her passenger side door and got in.

"Oh, that's all I am? His friend?" I said sounding fake hurt.

"Boy, shut up. You know what I meant".

"A book? This nigga don't even read".

"That's what I said!" Autumn said laughing. They continued

to make small talk while I took in her appearance. She looked like she'd been running around with an oversized t-shirt on and some leggings. It was a basic fit, but still looked good from what I could see. I was trying to take it all in, but I couldn't see her for real since it was damn near dark out and she was sitting down. I know one thing, whatever perfume or lotion she had on smelled good as fuck.

"Damn, this is why I don't fuck with niggas. Can't even support without them talking shit. Where the fuck my books at?" I said jokingly.

"Boy don't fucking do that" she giggled. She reached behind me and grabbed two books then handed them to me.

"Naw nigga, sign this shit!" I said giving them back to her.

"You bossy as fuck for no reason" she playfully rolled her eyes.

"I'm a boss baby, what you expect?"

"Shut the fuck up. You ain't shit".

"Damn, that's how you feel?" I joked, grabbing my chest.

"You're dramatic as fuck, you know that?" she grabbed a pen from her center console and then wrote some shit in the book and handed it back to me. I looked at her and then looked on the inside of the book where she signed her name.

"You know I'm probably not about to read this shit, but I had to support you. How much?"

"$20" she told me. "Thank you for the support, I appreciate it".

"Always".

Autumn

Seeing Durrell was weird after all this time. Not that it was a bad feeling, I just couldn't describe it. Also, seeing Isaiah and his other friend Brandon, it brought back the times when the four of us used to chill at my house. My Mama used to work until 9 and sometimes 10 pm so I would literally be at the house by myself all day. Me, being the fast little girl that I was, wanted to have my boyfriend and my brothers over, so I did. A lot. We couldn't help but build a bond. Even though over the years me, Isaiah and Brandon didn't really talk like that, it was all love whenever we did speak to each other.

I grabbed the kids from Malcolm's and made my way home. I was tired to say the least, but today was very productive. Most of my paperback copies of my books were gone, which I didn't expect to happen. *I really should start doing this more often,* I thought to myself. Really, I need to get back to writing and release something new. I haven't published anything in almost a year. COVID would've been the perfect time to drop something. Everyone was at home doing nothing, they would've loved to pick up a book and read. I missed that opportunity though, but it's all good. I'd get back to it sooner than later.

After getting the kids bathed and in the bed, I finally had some time to myself before I had to get up for work in the morning. I laid down and grabbed my phone scrolling through TikTok. I didn't want to download this damn app at first, but I had to admit, it was super entertaining. I could get lost in this shit, laughing for hours without even realizing it.

***

Father's Day weekend was coming to an end, and really, I was ready to go home. I decided to go see my dad who lives a few hours away in Ohio. I had a good time fishing and hanging out with him and the boys. Now, it was time to get back to my regular life.

Being on the road always brought me peace. I was able to do whatever I needed to do to get my mental together. Cry, sing my heart out, talk to God. It was nothing but me and the open road. Of course, my kids loved to interrupt my car concerts, but for the most part, it calmed me. *Ding!* I heard the sound of the messenger app go off.

Durrell: You back in the city?

Autumn: On the road. I'll be back in about 30-45 minutes.

Durrell: Pull up

Autumn: I gotta drop my kids off, but I will after that

Durrell: Ok, let me know

Durrell and I had been casually talking here and there since the day he bought the books from me. It was nothing major, just some harmless flirting. It felt good to get the attention of someone other than Malcolm. It also didn't hurt that we had history.

I made it back to the city and to my house in record time. I quickly changed my clothes and rushed back out of the house to drop the kids off at Malcolm's Dad's house for the night. I was grateful they called and asked for the boys because I could use a night to myself.

Durrell texted me the address and I realized that I was going to the east side yet again. This nigga wasn't even from the east side but stayed over there. After about 20 minutes of driving, I pulled up to the address he gave me then let him know I was here. I saw him walk out of the front door and on to the porch, and I had to admit, he looked good.

He was an even 6 feet, cocky, but still had a slight baller belly, a full beard with the perfect size lips and these doe shaped eyes that always made me feel like he was staring into my soul. That damn stare he did has always worked on me, even at 14. He had on his hood nigga starter pack: a white tee, basketball shorts and some Nike slides. I was damn near positive that his gun was tucked behind his back.

I got out of the car and walked up to the porch where him and a couple other people that I've never met stood. I felt eyes on me the closer I got to him.

"This you, nephew?" the older gentleman that was beside him said.

"It will be" he said licking his lips. He extended his arm for me to grab his hand and I caught a glimpse of his tattoos. *Imma end up fucking this man*, I thought to myself. I grabbed his hand and he pulled me in for a hug. Instinctively, I wrapped my arms around his neck as he wrapped his arms around my waist and squeezed me. The scent of his cologne invaded my nostrils. I couldn't help but take a quick but deep breath before he let me go.

"You look good as hell! Damn!" he said.

"Thank you! Thank you!" I said giggling as he spun me around admiring the sundress that I threw on.

"You want something to drink?"

"Yeah, what y'all got?" I asked. He led me into the house where he introduced me to a few people that were sitting in the living room playing a video game on the TV and then introduced me to more people that were in the kitchen. I wasn't paying a bit of attention to anyone else around me.

"You want some wine or you want liquor?" he asked. "Do you even drink?"

"Don't do that. I drink a little, just not dark".

"You know that's all I drink baby, you shit out of luck with that. I'll get you some wine" he said and went into the kitchen to fill my cup. Once he was done, he handed it to me and I took a sip.

"So, what's been going on Autumn? I can't believe you really pulled up on me".

"Why wouldn't I?"

"I ain't think you fucked with me like that?"

"Why you think that?" I asked with a frown. He shrugged his shoulders, took a sip of his drink and looked at me.

"I knew you was married and shit, I thought you was being respectful of your relationship". I chuckled.

"I was never married nigga".

"Stop cappin".

"I wasn't" I giggled and playfully rolled my eyes.

"What you call it then?"

"I was engaged, but we never actually got married".

"Shit y'all was together so long. Might as well have gotten married".

"Whatever" she waved me off. Aye, you know your friend was in my inbox. I thought it was a little weird, but this was before we were talking so I couldn't really bring it to you".

"What friend?" he asked with his eyebrow raised.

"Isaiah". I watched his face frown slightly.

"What did he say?" I pulled out my phone and showed him the DMs of Isaiah asking if I wanted to go to breakfast and catch up. He studied the phone for what seemed like forever and then handed it back to me.

"Imma talk to him about that shit". His jaws were clenched and I noticed his fist were balled up. I placed my hand on his shoulder and immediately released his fist.

"Is it that serious?"

"Yeah, I don't really like that shit".

"Why?"

"You know why. You off limits and he know that shit".

"You don't have to worry about that. At least not on my side. I would never fuck with none of your friends" I said honestly.

Before I could say anything else, he turned so that he was directly in front of me and placed his hands around my neck looking at me with such a serious expression, I was almost scared. He squeezed my neck slightly as we both looked in each other's eyes.

"You better fucking not. I'll fuck you up Autumn. On God" he said in a deep, sexy voice. I felt like I should be a little scared, but I wasn't. Actually, I was turned on and if all these people weren't in this house, I'd probably be kissing him right now. Instead of doing that, I smirked and moved my head forcing him to release the grip that he had on my neck.

"Boy, ain't nobody thinking about your friends".

"Yeah alright" he said and turned his attention towards one of the guy's who'd called his name. While his back was turned, I just stared at him. Ain't no way in hell I was feeling like this about this man. *I'm about to get myself into some shit.*

I don't know why I felt a way when Autumn showed me those messages from Isaiah, but I wanted to beat that nigga's ass. He introduced me to this damn girl, he knew first-hand how I felt about her. I didn't want to think my mans would snake me like that, but I've seen it done before. Still, I was going to let it go, at least for now.

"I'm hot. Can we go outside for a minute? My hair sweating out" Autumn asked me. She was so beautiful. After all these years, her little ass still did something to me. The shit was kind of scary. I nodded my head in response to her question, grabbed her hand and led her outside.

"This you?" I heard from behind me. I turned around to see this one girl standing there with one of her friends. I knew her from around the way. I couldn't think of her name for the life of me, but every time I saw her, she'd try to flirt and shoot her shot, but she wasn't my type. Not that she was ugly or anything, she was a decent looking chick. She just didn't have shit that I wanted.

I ignored her question and focused my attention on Autumn who was texting away on her phone, oblivious to the girls behind us.

"You telling the group chat about me?" I asked. She looked up at me and smiled. She had a cute ass, innocent smile, but I could also see something in her eyes. I couldn't pinpoint what it was, but I'm sure I'd figure it out the more I talked to her. One thing we never had a problem with was communicating with one another. We gave each other real ass, unfiltered advice, whether we wanted to hear that shit or not. For that reason alone, she'd forever hold a special place in my heart. That, and she took a nigga's virginity. I ain't gon never forget that.

"Ain't nobody talkin' about yo ass" she said giggling, putting her phone away.

"Yeah whatever".

We stood around on the porch laughing and joking. I even refilled her cup. It felt good to be around her. Her energy made me feel calm. I haven't felt that in so long, especially dealing with Rochelle on and off. A lot of that shit was my fault, but damn, she took things too far.

"Rell" I heard a female's voice say behind me.

"Wassup?"

"Do you be calling bitches bitches?" she asked.

"Not all bitches" I said and chuckled. Autumn rolled her eyes and laughed.

"So do you call *your* bitches, bitches?" This time it was the first girl who spoke to me. She put an emphasis on your. I blew out a breath of frustration and looked at her, noticing that she was looking at Autum who was looking at me waiting on me to respond.

"Nah. Only the ones that deserve it". Autumn laughed from behind me. They both looked liked they wanted to say something else, and I was mentally preparing myself for some bullshit. I've never seen Autumn fight, but that didn't mean she didn't have hands.

"We got a problem?" a deep voice asked. I turned my head towards the voice and saw some random nigga I ain't never seen before looking between me and the girls like he wanted smoke.

"Baby we're good" the second girl said.

"Nah, I keep hearing the word bitch being flung around. I know ain't nobody over here talking to my girl crazy".

Deciding that I'd heard enough, I grabbed Autumn's hand and gently pulled it to let her know to follow me. We walked down the porch steps and as we walked past, the nigga purposely bumped into me.

"Chill the fuck out bro. If I wanted to call yo bitch a bitch I would've. Be cool" I told him. I attempted to walk away until I heard him mumble "pussy ass nigga" under his breath. Without thinking twice, I dropped Autumn's hand and turned around, fist balled, ready for whatever.

"Come again?" I asked.

"Pussy ass nigga" the nigga repeated, getting in my face. I dropped Autumn's hand.

"What the fuck you wanna do bro?"

"Durrell, it's not that deep" I heard Autumn say, but at the moment, I was seeing read.

"Listen to yo bitch pus.." without warning, I sent a right hook to that nigga's left jaw. He stumbled back a bit, but quickly recovered from the blow, landing one of his own.

"I'm a pussy, but I bet that bitch on the porch hit harder than yo bitch ass" I said taunting him. That clearly triggered him. He rushed towards me and tackled me to the ground.

"Man, these niggas out here fighting!"

"Get the fuck off of him!" I heard a female scream. Regaining my strength, I pushed his ass off of me and stood to my feet where we continued to go blow for blow for about 30 more seconds before a few people came out and broke up the fight.

"Man, what the fuck was that!?" one of my homies asked me pulling me away from the house and walking down the street.

"Nigga I don't know. That nigga got in his feelings about that one bitch on the porch and it went from there" I explained trying to calm myself down. After a few minutes, I regained my composure and started looking around for Autumn, but I didn't see her anywhere.

"Aye, you seen Autumn?"

"Who is Autumn? Shorty you was with?" he asked and I nodded my head. "She quietly got the fuck on as soon as y'all started fighting" he chuckled. "She ain't want no parts of that shit".

Damn, I fucked up my chance.

<h1 style="text-align:center">Autumn</h1>

"Girl, that shit was crazy as hell!" I said giggling with my best friend Paris. I was filling her in on yesterday's crazy ass events.

"Yo scary ass got the fuck on" she laughed.

"Man, for starters, he had me on the eastside. I love my life. Soon as I sense danger, I'm getting the fuck on. I do not care!"

"You're a piece of shit. Just left that man".

"He wasn't by himself! He knew people!" I said still laughing.

"Aye, at least you know he ain't no hoe" she said and I rolled my eyes as if she could see me.

"While that may be true, that fight was unnecessary as fuck".

"Aye, unnecessary to you, but niggas are wired different".

"VERY different".

We continued to talk for a few more minutes before hanging up. Looking at the clock, I realized I needed to clock back in to work. My job was fairly easy, but I still hated talking to these customers, even through chat. They got ballsy when they were behind a keyboard.

I was just about done with my shift when I heard the Facebook Messenger alert tone. I glanced at my phone and smiled when I saw the message was from Durrell.

Durrell: You ain't talking to me?

Me: Did I say that?

Durrell: You ain't said nothing since yesterday.

Me: It's not that I'm not talking to you. I was gonna check on you and see if yo crazy ass was ok. Are you ok? Psycho

Durrell: I'm sorry you had to see that. I'm not crazy, you was there, you seen what happened.

Me: It's ok. You didn't know that was going to happen.

Durrell: Guess you really can't take the hood out a nigga

Me: No you can not. Especially not you lmao

Durrell: Well Ima come see you next time. I'm embarrassed. But girl I think you look better than when we were kids

Me: I would hope so. I was 14.

Durrell: Yeah, I said damn she fine as hell!

Me: Don't gas me

Durrell: Dead ass, and I had you catching a vibe and sipping wine. I'm sick

Me: Boy you gave me a fourth cup of wine like I'm a baby

Durrell: Lol what's your number?

Me: 3136777868

Durrell: Wow not you still got the same number

Me: Fuck you

Durrell: Imma call you in a minute

***

It had been about a week since I gave Durrell my number and we've been talking almost non-stop every day. The conversation flowed so easily with us. It was like I was talking to one of my friends. Well, he is one of my friends so I guess it's not that weird. We stayed up for hours talking about our past relationships, reminiscing on the past and even talking about what we wanted for our futures.

Finally, I could say that life was good and I'm actually happy. Even Malcolm and I were on decent terms. He hadn't mentioned the girl that MJ told me about, but MJ also hasn't mentioned her since that day so maybe it was nothing. Either way, I needed to have a conversation with him about who was and who wasn't allowed around our kids if we were both going to be dating. In my opinion, if it was nothing serious, they didn't need to meet the kids. Can't be having any and everybody around your babies.

"What are you over there thinking about?" Malcolm asked snapping me out of my thoughts.

"My bad, nothing major". He came by to grab the boys for the weekend, but forgot that my nephew was here for the weekend, visiting from Texas. Armon was driving me up a wall with his whining and crying the past few days. Mommy needed a break, but I could wait a couple more days.

After Malcolm left, I blasted some music and started cleaning up. I'd been cleaning so long, I didn't even realize that it had gotten dark outside. I knew if I sat down then I'd lose my momentum so I kept going. I was in the zone when my music was interrupted and my phone rang. Walking over to it, I saw that Durrell was facetiming me.

"Hello?"

"Damn you fine as hell" he said and I blushed.

"Boy whatever, I look a mess".

"Nah, you don't. What you doing?"

"Cleaning. You?"

"Chilling. On the west, thinking about you".

"Damn you west and you ain't even come see me? I knew you didn't fuck with me".

"What the hell you think I'm calling you for?"

"Who said you could come to my house?" I asked snickering.

"Girl, stop playing with me. I'll be there in 10 minutes".

"Ok, you need my address?"

"Autumn don't play with me. You know I know where you stay".

"I could have moved".

"Bye silly" he said and disconnected the call. Immediately, I ran upstairs to my room and looked myself over in the mirror.

I felt like I looked crazy but cute at the same time. My hair was in a ponytail with some gray shorts that made my ass look fatter and a gray t-shirt. I didn't really have time to change so I just said fuck it. I checked my pits to make sure I wasn't musty and also did a check on my coochie. Not that I planned on using it, but still...better safe than sorry. I also quickly sprayed a few dabs of my favorite perfume behind my ears and on my wrists. Just as I was walking out of the room, my phone vibrated with a text from Durrell saying that he was outside.

For a second, I forgot that MJ and my nephew were downstairs wide awake. Looking at the time, I saw that it was almost midnight. They'd be sleep eventually. I went into the den and saw that MJ was knocked out on the couch, but my nephew was still awake. He was so busy playing the game that he didn't even notice me standing there. I quietly backed away. If he knew I was awake he'd definitely be calling my name every 5 minutes. I couldn't have that.

I walked outside and saw Durrell's car in the driveway. He hopped out the car and I felt a tingling sensation down below. The man was fine and it was starting to piss me off because who told you to look like that? He had on a white tee with black basketball shorts, a pair of Nike slides and a white gold chain hanging from his neck. He smiled when we locked eyes, causing me to smile back.

"What's the deal gorgeous" he said extending his arms for a

hug. I wasted no time walking into his embrace. The smell of his cologne ingulfed my nose, further increasing the tingling feeling between my legs.

"Hey" I said shyly.

"You smell good as hell" he said.

"Thank you". We stood there talking about any and everything. Once the initial nerves wore off, I found myself opening up to him even more about my relationship with Malcolm, where I am now and what I want moving forward. He even opened up a bit about his relationship with his baby mama. It seemed like we were in the same headspace.

"You ain't fucked nobody since your baby daddy?" he asked and I shook my head.

"Nah. I don't have nobody to fuck" I said slightly chuckling. "I mean, I would spin the block on somebody I already fucked but it has to be the right person". I made sure to make eye contact with him when I said that. "It can't just be anybody. Plus, I don't want any new bodies and I don't want mothafuckas to know where I live".

"They don't have to know where you live. You can go to them" he said not getting the hint.

"I could, but I don't think I'm ready for that. I'd feel like they're trying to kill me or something". This time it was his turn to chuckle.

"Girl ain't nobody gon kill yo little ass".

"You don't know that! They might want to keep me all to themselves and the moment I try to escape I'm dead" I said being dramatic. He looked at me, laughed, and shook his head.

"Nah you trippin. I mean, they might wanna keep you all to themselves. Shit, I know I would want to" he said licking his lips, staring at me intensely. That damn stare always did something to me.

"Oh, you would?" I flirted.

"I would. Now, who you tryna spin the block on if it ain't you baby daddy. You ain't got that many exes" he said inching closer to me.

"This one nigga I know. I just recently started talking to him again. I think I might like him a little bit".

"Damn just a little bit? I think you should like somebody more than that if you're trying to give your body to him".

"You're right. Maybe it is more than a little, but he doesn't need to know that. Once they know how much you like them, they use that to their advantage and start acting weird. That's also how you get your feelings hurt".

"Who the fuck is they?" he asked now inches away from my face. The intensity of the stare was getting me hot and bothered and I wanted to look away so bad, but I couldn't. I didn't want this moment to go away. My body was craving this man. The connection we had was so electrifying that it was scary. He leaned his head in towards mine and my breathing quickened.

"Autumn" he said in a deep voice, barely above a whisper. "I want you".

Without another word being said, his lips were on mine. The kiss sent shock waves through my body. I damn near felt like I was floating. I've never in my life felt like this and it scared me, but it also intrigued me.

"Mmm" I said letting a moan escape my lips as he deepened our kiss. He wrapped his arms around my waist and I locked my arms around his neck. We continued to devour each other for about sixty seconds before he pulled away and took a few steps back. We gazed at each other, both breathing heavily.

"This is bad".

"Why is it bad?"

"I don't think we should be doing this?"

"Why not?"

"Me and you together has always been something we can't control or explain. Do you agree?"

"I do".

"If we go down this road it ain't no turning back. Are you ready for that?" he asked. I stepped towards him and pulled his shirt towards my body.

"Do you want this?" I asked.

"You have no idea how bad".

"Then you should probably stop talking" I said and led him inside the house.

Durrell

This is exactly how her aggressive ass took my virginity, I thought as I watched her ass cheeks sway from side to side going up the steps. It was a déjà vu moment for me, although I know she didn't remember. The day I lost my virginity will forever play in my head. I don't remember what we were doing leading up to it, but I do remember her ass grabbing my hand and leading me up the steps just like she was doing now. I was nervous. Something was telling me this wasn't a good idea, but I couldn't stop it if I tried. Autumn had always been my weakness, since the first day I laid eyes on her, and I couldn't begin to explain why. She had some type of voodoo hold on me or something. She could get anything from me and I think she knew that shit.

When we got to her room, I took in the décor. Her bed was big as hell, with a big ass headboard and what looked like benches around the sides, matching the headboard. The shit was sweet as hell. She had two night-stands on each side of the bed, a black dresser with candles, a tv and what looked like some lotion and other girly shit on it. She also had a beauty mirror or some shit in the corner. It looked like a desk, but it had a mirror with lights around it and a bunch of her girly make up, hair products, lashes, flat irons and shit. But the vibe was cool and it smelled good as hell in here. I noticed the candle burning on the dresser.

"Oh, yo lil ass set me up" I said smirking.

"What you mean?" she asked sitting on the bed. I pointed to the candle and she giggled, making my dick jump.

"Naw, I didn't set you up crazy. I always light a candle after I finish cleaning up or just when I'm in the mood. It calms me. Plus, it smells amazing".

"Not better than you though" I told her and she bit her small bottom lip. Everything this girl did turned me on.

"Come here" she said in a low, sexy voice. Without hesitation, I walked over to her, placing my body in front of hers. She opened her legs so that I could get in between. I kissed her, slowly backing her down onto the bed. *I can't believe this shit is about to happen.*

We kissed intensely until I pulled away and helped her remove her shirt and shorts. The sight before me made my heart skip a beat. She had on a black lace bra with the matching black lace panties. A thong at that. I haven't seen this girl naked in twelve years, so to see her grown woman body did something to me. I've never been this turned on by someone in my life. I looked at her, looking back at me with those sexy ass eyes. I could tell we were on the same page. She wanted this just as bad as I did, if not more. No words needed to be spoken.

I stood up and took my shirt off, never breaking eye contact with her. I then took my shorts and draws off at the same time. Her eyes got so damn big, she almost looked scared, but she quickly recovered. She removed her bra and then her panties. Her titties were the perfect size and there was no sagging, even after two kids. I couldn't wait to suck on them. Don't even get me started on her thick ass thighs, and that small gut she was so self-conscious about.

"Damn" I said barely above a whisper. She scooted back on the bed and spread her legs showing me her bald pussy. My dick was so hard it felt like my shit was about to break. I started to come towards her, but then remembered the most important thing. Quickly grabbing my shorts off the floor, I reached in the pocket and grabbed a condom. I didn't expect for this shit to happen tonight, but I always kept a condom on me because you just never know. This moment proved that.

I quickly put the condom on my dick and made my way towards her.

"Are you sure?" I asked one last time. She looked at me, nodded her head yes, then grabbed the back of my neck bringing my head down to kiss her. While we kissed, I slowly inserted myself inside her center.

Just entering the tip inside of her made me want to buss. Her pussy was already soaked and it was tight, so I know she wasn't lying when she said she hadn't had sex with anybody since her baby daddy. I took pride in knowing I would be the only person outside of him that she gave herself to in the last ten years.

I noticed she tensed up a little as I made my way completely inside of her.

"Ahh" she moaned in my ear. I slowly pushed myself in and out of her, trying my best to concentrate on anything other than how good this felt. I don't know what I expected, but this was better than anything I could have ever dreamed of. Her pussy clamped around my dick like it was made for me.

"Shit Autumn" I said feeling a tingling sensation flow through my body. I've never felt that shit before. Finally, I found my rhythm and began beating her shit up, causing her to moan loudly and call my name.

"Oh my God this feels so good" she cried in pleasure. Hearing her say that made me want to give her the whole world. If she asked me for a kidney right now, I'd cut myself open and give it to her. This shit was dangerous. Not to mention, I had a condom on. If the shit felt this good with a condom, I could just imagine how it was hitting if I went in raw. I grabbed her legs and pulled them up on my shoulders and then plummeted myself into her.

"OH FUCK!" she cried digging her nails into my back. That shit stung a little bit but I didn't give a fuck. I wanted her to feell what she'd been missing all these years. I wasn't a little kid anymore. I'm a grown ass man. "Durrell, please".

"Please what?" I asked still drilling her.

"Don't stop. Don't stop. I'm bouta cum" she cried. Per her request, I kept on drilling until I felt her muscles tighten. "Ahhhhhhhh shit!!" she yelled.

Looking down at her, I damn near couldn't control myself. She made the sexiest love faces I'd ever seen. Her eyes were closed, eyebrows furrowed, biting her bottom lip.

"Fuck Autumn, you're so fucking beautiful" I told her, meaning every single word. "Damn. Fuck!" I said unable to control it any longer. I released my load into the condom, still inside her. Slowly, I pulled out and just stared at her breathing heavily. She looked up at me and smiled reaching her arms out for me. I accepted the invitation, leaning towards her and kissed her.

"You're dangerous. You know that right?" I said after we broke the kiss.

"How?" she asked playing dumb.

"Girl, I see why that man was with you for ten fucking years" I stated and she giggled.

"Yeah, well he was cheating on me for 6 of those years so..." she said and her voice trailed off. I could tell that her baby daddy was still a sore subject, and I felt bad for even bringing it up.

"My bad, Autumn. That shit still got you feeling a way?" I rolled off of her and laid on my back, looking up at the ceiling. She sat up and straddled me. I swear she was so fucking gorgeous and she didn't even know it.

"I mean, I think a part of me will always feel a way about it because of how much that shit hurt me and because of the timing of everything, but I'm ok for real. I'm ready to move on" she said and I nodded my head believing every word. One thing about this girl, she has never lied to me no matter how bad she thought I might react. That quality was rare to find in any female, let alone a female from Detroit, so she got my utmost respect.

"Oh, you're trying to move on, huh?"

"Yup" she stated proudly. I chuckled. Before I could respond, she leaned over and kissed me, instantly making my dick hard again. Once she felt my manhood against her, she broke the kiss and looked at me. "That's how you feel?"

"You wanna find out?" I asked smirking. In one quick motion she lifted up and then came back down onto my shaft. "Got damn!" I said realizing she was still soaking wet. This the shit that was going to have my ass in love, and I wasn't ready for any of it.

Autumn

"Mommy, why you so happy?" MJ asked as he came down the steps. I was at my desk, working with the music blasting like I usually did, but my son knew me better than almost anybody.

"Dang, Mommy can't be happy?"

"You can, I'm just asking" he said and walked off.

I couldn't tell my baby that I'd just gotten the best dick I ever had in my life. He would've been looking at me like I was crazy. However, I will say I completely understand why bitches fight over dick. Sometimes that shit is worth it. What I got last night definitely made me a believer. I was expecting him to have some good dick, but that right there...baby! I had to tell somebody, so, in true female fashion, I texted the group chat.

Me: I had sex last night

Paris: Huh? With who???? If you say Malcolm, I'll beat yo ass

Me: Lmao NO

Raegan: Who? The ex you told us you been talking to?

Me: Yes

Paris: *sends shocked emoji*

Raegan: OH OK!! HOW WAS IT?!

Paris: *emphasizes Raegan's message*

Me: That shit was amazing!

Paris: Bitch I told you! I told you it was way better dick out here than yo fuckin baby daddy!

Me: *laughs at Paris' message*

Raegan: Are you gonna do it again?

Me: HELL YEAH

We continued to talk in the group chat until work started getting busy. Before I knew it, lunch time was here. I made everyone something to eat, and just as I was about to sit down and eat, my phone rang.

"Hello?"

"If you hitting and quitting you can just say that" Durrell said on the other end. I laughed.

"You retarded. Why would I be hitting and quitting Durrell?"

"Yo ass ain't show me no love when I left and you ain't texted me all day" he said and I chuckled.

"Boy I hugged you. I was trying to get you out before MJ or my nephew saw you, and I haven't texted yo ass yet because I'm working".

"Ok yeah you right. What time you off?"

"7:30".

"What you doing after you get off?"

"Nothing, dropping off my nephew and then dropping off the kids with their dad".

"Can I come back over?" he asked. My lips curled up into a smile.

"Look at you, addicted already".

"Let me tell you, that shit right there girl. I'll die bout it" he joked and I let out a hearty laugh.

"Durrell please!"

"You laughing, I'm dead ass. Just say the word" he said in a serious tone.

"Calm down psycho, you ain't gotta kill nobody".

"Just letting you know I will. But go ahead and finish your shift. I'll hit you up when I'm on the way" he said and we disconnected the call.

The rest of the work day went by smoothly. All I could think about was seeing Durrell later on. I dropped my nephew off and then made my way to Malcolm's apartment.

"Wassup baby mama" he greeted.

"What's poppin baby dad". He grabbed Armon out of the car seat and then grabbed the bag that was in the backseat.

"I'll see you on Sunday baby" I told MJ.

"Ok Mom, love you"

"I love you more".

"Alright then" Malcolm said and closed the door.

I watched them walk into the complex and then pulled off. Malcolm still hadn't bothered to mention anything about that girl, so I assumed it wasn't anything serious, but if my baby mentioned that she was around again, I was going to have to say something. I don't give a fuck who he dated, but I at least needed to meet the girl so I could point her out in a line up if I ever needed to.

I got back home, took a shower, changed clothes, straightened up all while waiting on Durrell to text or call me. I don't even remember dosing off, but I woke up to my phone vibrating against my arm.

"Hello?" I asked in a groggy tone.

"Damn you went to sleep on me?"

"Yeah, something like that?"

"You still want me to slide or you wanna get some sleep?"

"Nah you can come" I said quickly sitting up.

"Alright, I'm outside, open the door" he said disconnecting

the line. I hopped out the bed and went to open the front. There he was in all his chocolate fineness. "What's the deal sleepy head" he said walking up to me and embracing me in a warm hug. As usual, the scent of his cologne filled my nostrils and my knees became weak. He smelled so damn good. I wanted to say it was Gucci Guilty or Dior. Either way the smell was intoxicating.

We went upstairs to my room and chilled, watching Netflix and just talking. It was weird that I felt this way so quickly. I mean, we had history, but still, we hadn't really talked in years. It was throwing me off how well we connected. The chemistry that we had was effortless and unlike anything I'd ever felt before. I felt safe in his presence, wanted, and really, that's all any woman wanted from a man.

"I wanna take you out" he blurted out and I smiled. "I'm serious. It's been almost two months since we've been kicking it and I haven't had a chance to take you out yet. That shit ain't cool. Imma let you know the date in enough time for you to get a baby sitter and then Imma show you a good time. Cool?"

"I hope you don't think I'm about to say no to that" I giggled cuddling up next to him.

"I wasn't really asking for your approval. I was asking to make sure you understood the plan".

I looked up at him and saw the seriousness in his eyes. The more I stared, the more my love box craved him. He licked his lips and slightly bit on his bottom lip, turning me on even more.

"Durrell" I called out.

"Yeah?"

"Take your clothes off". Without hesitation, I watched as he slowly got off the bed and began to take his clothes off. Once he was naked, I observed his dark chocolate skin and perfect, chocolate manhood. My mouth watered just looking at it.

"Come here" I said summoning him with my index finger. He walked back over to the bed and laid down on his back. Now, it was my turn to take my clothes off, never breaking eye contact with him.

"Damn" I heard him mumble once I was completely naked. I walked over to the bed and crawled on top of him, then leaned down to kiss him. Slowly, I broke our kiss and trailed my kisses down from his neck to his chest, going lower towards my personal snickers bar. "Wait". He said grabbing my shoulders. I frowned and looked up at him.

"Wait for what?"

"You don't have to do this". Again, I frowned.

"Trust me, if I didn't want to do this, I wouldn't be doing it".

"I know, it's just..." he hesitated. "You ain't never done this with me before".

"First time for everything baby" I said smirking.

I knew he was hesitant. He didn't think I really knew how to give head, but little did he know, I'd learned some things. Granted, the only dick I've ever sucked is Malcolm's, I like to think he taught me well. I never really liked giving head with him though, because I felt like he didn't deserve it after all the cheating. But this was different. I was doing this because I really wanted to, not out of obligation.

Reaching my destination, I opened my mouth and slowly took his penis in. He moaned slightly as I covered his entire shaft. I swirled my tongue around, as I slowly began to bob my head up and down while stroking him. I repeated the motion a few times before stopping and focusing my attention on the head of his dick.

"Got damn Autumn" he grunted.

I moaned softly while still swirling my tongue around and then deep throated his shaft. His verbal praises turned me on in a way that was unfamiliar to me. I continued to suck this man's dick like my life depended on it. I wanted him to feel how he made me feel. After a few minutes, I felt his dick twitch in my mouth so I knew he was close to finishing. I released his manhood from my mouth and sat up straight.

"Not yet" I told him in a low voice. He looked a little confused, but didn't argue with me. In one swift motion, I straddled him and sat down on his shaft. I couldn't help but let out a gasp as I took all of him in. Slowly, I lifted myself up and down, riding him as if I was riding a horse.   "Shit". We continued to curse each other in pleasure as I sped up my pace. Durrell began thrusting his pelvis from under me.

"Fuck!" I cried.

After a few minutes I started to feel a tingling sensation and knew I was about to reach my climax. I opened my eyes, looking directly at Durrell whose eyes were already trained on me.

"You look so fucking beautiful riding this dick" he praised in a low, sexy tone.

I leaned down, kissing him passionately. We broke our kiss and I sat up, slowing down my pace as I reached my peak. Durrell extended his arm and wrapped his hand around my neck, gripping it slightly.

"Mmmhmm, I feel you baby. Good girl. Daddy right there with you". That was all I needed to hear as I released my juices onto his shaft.

"Shit!" we both cried as we came together.

We both were frozen in time for a moment, staring at each other.

"Come here" he said. Leaning down, we kissed again. Although we'd just had an amazing session, I still felt the sparks between us as our tongues danced together. I broke away from the kiss and slowly climbed off of him, positioning myself on my back right next to him. We were silent, but no words needed to be spoken in that moment. After a few moments, he chuckled lowly.

"What's funny?" I asked looking over at him.

"You never cease to amaze me" he said smirking.

"What did I do?"

"Girl what didn't you do!? That shit right there was amazing. I gotta stay away from you for a few days". This time it was my turn to chuckle.

"For what?"

"You can't keep putting that shit on me like that Autumn. It's another side to me".

"I know it is. I wanna see it" I said teasing him.

"Yeah, you say that shit now" he said smiling.

"You thought I didn't know how to suck dick didn't you?"

"Well, yeah! Last time I checked yo ass was like 'you want me to put my mouth on that'?!" he said mocking me.

"First of all, that shit was damn near fifteen years ago. I'm grown as hell now".

"You ain't gotta tell me baby, you just proved that. Go ahead grown ass". I playfully smacked his arm. "Malcolm ass taught you well. I'm so happy he cheated on yo ass".

"Why are you happy about that!?" I frowned.

"If he didn't, you would still be with him which means this right here" he said pointing between me and him, "wouldn't have happened. So yeah, I'm happy that shit happened because I got my second chance with you".

"Awww you're so cute" I said kissing his face.

"Don't ruin the moment now" he said wrapping his arms around my waist.

We playfully fought for a few minutes before I realized what time it was and insisted, we go to sleep. He fought me for a minute, claiming he wasn't sleepy, but five minutes later he was snoring.

<h1 style="text-align:center">Malcolm</h1>

"If you aren't fucking her, then why can't I meet her?" Bianca asked for what seemed like the fifth time today. I ran my hand down my face, tired of having this conversation. Whenever she wanted to argue, she brought up my baby mama. It was getting old really quick.

"Because I'm not ready for you to meet her yet. How many times do I have to tell you that?"

"Why not? It's been three months. I've been around your kids, why can't I meet their Mom if it ain't shit going on like you say?"

"I'll talk to her about it, ok?" I tried to reason with her. At this point, I'd say anything to get her to shut the fuck up.

"She doesn't even know you have a girlfriend, does she? You probably haven't said shit about me" she continued to fuss, shaking her head.

"Why does it matter? She got a whole nigga she fucking with!" I said raising my voice.

Autumn and I talked a few times and she let it be known that it was going to be someone around our kids. I couldn't really say shit since Bianca had been around the kids without her knowing. Plus, the nigga that she was fucking with wasn't a new nigga, so I trusted her judgement. I didn't necessarily trust that nigga, but I couldn't do shit about that. I always knew she would either turn into a hoe or go back to one of her old niggas when we broke up. I used to say it all the time and she thought I was trippin, now look at her.

"You said that shit like you're mad because she moved on?" she said then paused. "Ahhh, ok, I get it. She doesn't want yo ass and now you're mad. Do you still have feelings for her Malcolm?"

"Oh my fucking God. Listen, I was with her ass for ten years. I'm not going to sit and act like that shit just went away. Do I want to be with her? No. If I did, I wouldn't be with you! I'm where I want to be. You need to calm the fuck down. Just because shit ain't moving how you want it to move doesn't mean it won't happen".

"Yeah alright" she said storming off.

Bianca and I have been dating since April, and she's been hounding me for about a month now to meet Autumn.

She's lucky she even met the boys, and that was on accident. She popped up one day and they were here, so I just let her and her daughter come in and spend some time. The kids seemed to like her, especially Armon, so I just said fuck it and let her start coming around when I had them. Still, I hadn't talked to Autumn about her and I knew I was going to hear her mouth, especially since she was upfront and honest about Durrell.

I plopped down on the couch and sighed. Pulling out my phone, I decided to just go ahead and get it over with.

Me: Yo

BM: Wassup baby daddy?

I chuckled at the text. I was used to her calling me baby daddy, but I used to joke and say "keep calling me that and that's all Imma be". Spoke that shit into existence.

Me: Shit. I wanted to talk to you about something. You free to talk when I drop the boys off?

BM: Yeah, that's cool. Everything ok?

Me: Yeah, nothing major

BM: Ok.

Placing my phone on the couch, I got up to tend to Bianca. I understood why she was so skeptical; she had every right to be. Not just because of me, but because of her past. She had been through a lot and I tried to show her that I cared and show her something different. Still, the girl was crazy as hell, but I loved that crazy shit, it showed she cared.

Pulling up to Autumn's house, I got the boys out, put them in the house and then grabbed their bags. Taking everything inside, I found Autumn in the living room, still at her desk.

"You still working?" I asked.

"Technically, no. I'm just finishing up" she said and I nodded my head.

She spun around in her office chair so that she was facing me. I couldn't act like her little ass wasn't still fine as hell. She was dressed casually in some biker shorts and a t-shirt, but she was still beautiful. I stared at her for a second, observing her milk chocolate complexion. If I didn't know any better, I'd say she was glowing. I'm genuinely happy for her. I know that I put her through a lot of shit over the years, the cheating, abuse, all that shit that she loves bringing up any chance she gets.

"So, what did you want to talk to me about?" she asked breaking me out of my thoughts.

"Right" I said clearing my throat.

For some reason, I was a little nervous. I guess I never thought that we'd be having this conversation. I just figured we'd always be together. Not saying that I wanted to get back with her, because I didn't, I was just used to certain shit when it came to us. Now, everything was different. Granted, it was for the best, it was just taking me some time to get used to it.

"I've been seeing somebody" I told her. I paused, waiting for her facial expression or body language to change, but it didn't.

"I know. I was wondering when you were finally going to tell me", she stated. I slightly frowned.

"How'd you know?"

"When are you gonna learn that you really aren't that sneaky Malcolm?" she chuckled. "A few months ago, when I came to pick up the boys, I saw a little girl in your window. When I pulled off MJ told me that he was playing with Daddy's friend's daughter and I asked was Daddy's friend a girl or a boy and he said a girl so I said oh" she said shrugging her shoulders. She seemed very unbothered and I didn't know how to take that. I expected her to get mad at me, but instead, she didn't give a fuck.

"Yeah. I wanted to tell you when she first came around the kids, but it was unexpected. Plus, I wanted to make sure shit was serious" I stated honestly. I saw her raise an eyebrow slightly.

"Oh, so it's serious? You really like her huh?" she asked and I nodded my head. "That's good Malcolm. I'm happy for you. So, what's her name? What does she do? When do I get to meet her? What does she look like?" she asked all in one breath.

"Damn, one at a time. Her name is Bianca. We work together, and you ain't meeting her right now". She frowned.

"Why not?"

"It ain't the right time".

"What kind of sense does that make? She can meet and spend time with my kids but she can't meet me?" I cringed slightly. She sounded exactly like Bianca.

"I'm just not comfortable with y'all meeting yet". She stared at me for a second, trying to read between the lines of what I'd just said. Suddenly, it was like a light bulb went off in her head.

"Our timelines overlap, don't they?"

"What you mean?"

"Boy, stop it. When we were still fucking around a little bit, you were fucking with her? If you were, it really doesn't matter. It's not like we're still fucking around right now. I just need to know the timeline so if it ever comes up, I know what to say" she stated with a straight face. I looked at her, confused. *Who the fuck is this girl? The Autumn I know would be tryna kill me right now. Damn, she really over me.*

"Not really, they don't overlap. We stopped fucking around like right before I moved, me and her didn't start dating until April" I told her. She nodded her head in approval.

"Okay, well we don't have anything to worry about then. Why don't you want us to meet? She doesn't like me or something?"

"Nah, it's not that. She doesn't know you to not like you. She wants to meet you too actually".

"Ok, so set it up, and do it soon. Stop being scary".

"Yeah, alright nigga. I'll see you in a few days when I come back to get them" I told her and she nodded turning her body back to her desk and getting back to work. I went upstairs and kissed my boys, said my goodbyes and walked out the house.

***

A few weeks had passed since that conversation with Autumn, and I was starting to feel like I was ready for them to meet. Shit was going to be awkward as hell, but fuck it, it was inevitable.

Me: Wyd

BM: Working, wassup?

Me: You wanna meet her?

BM: Yeah, when?

Me: Now

BM: What?

Me: FaceTime

BM: I'm working, but ok...

"Bae!" I called out. A few moments later she appeared in the doorway. "You wanna meet her?"

"Yeah, when?"

"Right now". She sat down on the bed next to me looking confused.

"What you mean right now?" I held up the phone. "FaceTime?" I nodded. "Yeah, sure". I unlocked my phone and dialed Autumn's number holding the camera up so our faces were visible.

After a few rings, the phone said connecting and Autumn's face appeared on the screen with a slight frown on her face, typing away on her keyboard. She had her natural shoulder length hair done with a part down the middle. In true Autumn fashion, she made sure her lashes were on and she was dressed. I used to ask her why she got dressed every day and she just said it made her feel good.

"Wassup baby mama?"
"What's poppin baby dad".

"Hey beautiful! What's wrong?" Bianca asked inserting herself in the conversation before I could properly introduce them.

"Hey, how are you? Nothing's wrong. I'm just working right now and this customer is irritating. I'm ok though" she said with a forced smile.

"Oh okay. I'm good".

"That's good" Autumn replied and then it grew silent.

"Umm, so yeah, I just wanted y'all to finally meet so y'all both can shut the fuck up".

"Boy shut the fuck up" they both said simultaneously. I shook my head.

"It's nice to put a face to the name"

"Oh, for real? What name is that?"

"Huh?" Autumn asked confused.

"You said it's nice to put a face to the name. What name?" Autumn laughed slightly.

"Girl, you know your name, I ain't gotta tell you". I looked at Bianca then at Autumn.

"Do you know my name? What's my name?" Bianca continued to ask. Autumn frowned.

"Yeah, you're being weird. It was nice meeting you. Imma get back to work" Autumn said and disconnected the call.

"You still gon sit here and tell me y'all ain't fucking?!" Bianca said snatching the phone out of my hand and throwing it across the room. Before I could react, she sent a blow to my right jaw.

"Man what the fuck is wrong with you!?" I shouted hopping off of the bed.

"What the fuck was her problem?"

"Her? Nigga do you see the way you just acted? That shit was unnecessary and you know it Bianca".

"How? Because I asked her what my name was? She had a problem from the moment she answered the phone. Don't act like you didn't see that".

"She said she was working and was irritated with a customer. It didn't have shit to do with you B. You doing too much. Calm yo ass down".

"Look at you being a good baby daddy taking up for her. You full of shit!" she yelled getting in my face.

"Bianca, don't start this shit with me today. I gave you what you wanted and you acted a fucking fool. Whose fault is that?!"

"I'm so fucking done with you Malcolm! I swear. You ain't never gonna tell the truth. Get the fuck out!" I wanted to argue back just to prove my point, but it was useless. She wasn't going to understand.

"Yeah, alright. I'll talk to you tomorrow bro" I said walking past her.

Just as I reached the doorway, something hard hit me in the back of my head. I spun around, looking at her with nothing but rage in my eyes. Without thinking twice, I charged towards her. Once I reached her, I grabbed her by her throat and squeezed.

"Are you fucking stupid!? Do you really wanna do this shit right now? Chill the fuck out before I kill yo dumb ass!" I screamed in her face. She tried her best to fight me, flailing her arms around trying to land punches.

"Get...the fuck...OFF ME!" she screamed.

Realizing I wasn't going to let her go, she stopped trying to fight me. I started to loosen my grip when I felt a sharp pain in my balls. I let go of her to grab my manhood, groaning in pain.

"Bitch are you fucking stupid! Don't ever put your bitch ass hands on me hoe!" she yelled sending a kick to my abdomen. I doubled over in pain as she began to land blow after blow to my back and head. I let her get a few good hits in before I regained some strength and got off the floor. Once I was on my feet, she tried to charge at me, but I grabbed her arm and twisted it slightly.

"Calm the fuck down Bianca!" I pulled her body towards mine and wrapped my arm around her so that I had her in a headlock.

"LET ME FUCKING GO!" she screamed still trying to fight.

"I'm not letting shit go until you calm yo ass down. I'm about to leave. Don't talk to me, don't say shit to me. You call me when you get your shit together. You hear me?" Unable to fight any longer, she nodded her head. I released my grip that I had on her and pushed her then walked out.

Autumn

A few days passed since I met Malcolm's weird ass girlfriend. He came over the next day to get the kids and we talked about it a little. He asked me my opinion of her and I expressed that I felt she was weird. Especially when she was trying to get me to say her name, trying to see if I would say the wrong name and catch Malcolm up in some bullshit. I didn't have time for their bullshit. He told me they got into it right after I hung up, which I expected. He said she feels like we're still fucking around and that I had an attitude from jump when I answered the phone, but I don't really give a fuck. I clearly explained that I was working which was the reason for my facial expression, but if that's not how she received it then oh well.

"What are you over there thinking about?" Paris asked me. Since I was kid free, I went out to eat with Paris and Raegan. We were currently at *Starter's* waiting on our drinks.

"Nothing, I'm good" I said shaking my head.

"Ok, so what happened after you met weirdo?" Paris asked.

"Nothing, I went about my day. I did tell Malcolm that she was weird to me and I thought she'd be cuter". Raegan laughed.

"You did not tell that man his girl was ugly".

"I didn't say ugly. I said I thought she'd be cuter and I felt like he could do better but whatever" I shrugged. They both started to laugh. "What?"

"You a mean ass bitch, that's what".

"How is that mean? I gave my honest opinion. He asked for

it!"

"What does she look like?" Paris asked.

"Not cute" I laughed. "I don't know how to describe her. I don't know none of her socials to show you".

We continued to talk and giggle, having a good time. While we were eating, my phone dinged indicating a notification. I grabbed it and saw it was Durrell texting asking if I was having a good time and if I was ready for our date in a few days. I smiled at my phone. In the past few months that I'd been fucking around with Durrell, I'd been happier than ever. I really had nothing to complain about. I had a great job, money in the bank, my kids were happy and healthy, great friends, me and my kid's dad were on good terms and I had a man who was treating me right and consistently dicking me down. Life was great!

After going back and forth with Durrell for a while, he let me know he'd be at my house later that night. I put my phone down and focused on whatever it was Paris and Raegan were chatting about. After a few minutes, I picked up my phone to show them something on Facebook. Opening the app, I realized I had a notification on messenger. Opening the messenger app, I saw the notification at the top right corner and quickly realized that whoever had messaged me wasn't friends with me. Going to the message, I let out a hearty laugh when I realized who it was.

"Y'all won't believe this shit!"

"What?" they both asked. I turned the phone around to face them on the other side of the booth.

"Who is this?" Paris asked looking at the message. She looked up at me waiting for an answer.

"Malcolm's girlfriend" I said still chuckling.

"Shut the fuck up!" Raegan exclaimed.

"Dead ass". Raegan passed the phone back to me and I reread the message.

Bianca Davidson: Bitch you tried it. You mad I snatched yo baby daddy hoe? Imma snatch yo new nigga since I'm so ugly and he could've did better bitch.

Under the message I saw that she'd called me on messenger three times back to back.

Me: Lmao. You're a weirdo. How can you snatch something I already threw away baby? My nigga wouldn't touch you with a ten-foot pole sweetheart. Stay safe

Bianca Davidson: Naw I'm ugly and he can do better, remember? Bitch how you younger and look older? Delusional ass hoe. Fuck you and Malcolm, y'all both weird and I'm done but bitch never ugly.

Me: Now you ugly, weird and hurt lmao. Good night

I showed Paris and Raegan and then proceeded to screenshot the messages to show Shani in the group chat.

"I'm sick Malcolm bitch ass went back and told her what you said" Paris said as we left the restaurant. I shrugged and hit the button to unlock my car doors.

"I don't give a fuck. I said what I said. What she gon do, beat my ass? She's clearly bothered by me and now that I know she feel some type of way about me, Imma make it worse. I want her to hate me". I said laughing. We said our goodbyes and I made my way to my man.

The night couldn't have ended on a better note. Food and drinks with my girls then back to my man for some good sex, I was on cloud nine. Durrell was sleeping peacefully, so I took the opportunity to roll over and grab my phone so I could scroll through social media. As soon as I picked up the phone, it lit up displaying almost thirty notifications from the group chat and five missed calls from Shani and Paris. Frowning, I checked the group chat.

Paris: This bitch got the right fucking one

Shani: She's a fucking weirdo and I wanna beat her ass. AUTUMN STOP SUCKING DICK FOR A SECOND AND LOOK AT THIS FUCKING PHONE

Instead of responding to the group chat, I FaceTimed so that I could talk to everybody at once.

"Damn bitch, we could've been dying!" Paris yelled as soon as she answered the phone.

"I hope you were having a good time because you're about to be mad as fuck" Shani told me.

"What the hell is going on?"

"That weird ass bitch done stalked your whole life, found me and Shani and has been writing us on Facebook since we left the restaurant" Paris told me. Again, I frowned.

"Saying what?"

"She said you're obsessed and jealous of her. You're a weak ass bitch, you don't want no smoke. She's going on and on about how she's not ugly and we need to relay the message. She told me and Shani that she'd rather talk to us instead of you because you goofy and Malcolm told her you weren't cut like that, but we are" Paris rambled.

"Excuse me?" I couldn't help but to let out a laugh.

"Then the bitch came in my inbox saying that we eating each other pussy and we're going to always stick up for you even when you're wrong. Just a whole bunch of bullshit".

"But here's where the hoe made me mad and where we had to bring you back into this" Paris said. She gave me a look like she really didn't want to say what she was about to tell me.

"Spit it out".

"That bitch said that she takes better care of your kids than you and they might as well be hers".

"EXCUSE ME!?" I yelled, forgetting that Durrell was laying

next to me sleeping. He hopped up, looking confused. "Oh, this bitch has me fucked up! You can say whatever about me but you can't say shit to me about my kids or my parenting".

"What are you talking about? What happened?" Durrell asked confused

"Hey cousin" Paris said to Durrell. They weren't really cousins, but they had the same last name so they started calling each other cousin.

"Hey friend" Shani greeted.

"What's the deal. What's wrong with you baby? What happened?"

I wanted to answer, but I couldn't. All I could do is sit there and think about all the different ways I could bash her skull in. I felt Durrell grab the phone from me and start talking to the girls, but I couldn't comprehend what was being said.

"Bestie!" Paris yelled snapping me out of my thoughts. I looked over at Durrell who was already looking at me with a concerned expression plastered across his face.

"Huh?"

"Are you ok?"

"No, I'm not. But I will be" I smiled.

"Why are you smiling?"

"Imma handle it y'all. Don't even trip. For now, Imma lay-up with my man and let her miserable ass think I'm a weak ass bitch. Trust me, I got it" I assured them. They didn't really believe me, but it was ok. It was clear she wanted to push my buttons, but I wasn't going to let her. Even though my kids were a trigger for me, I was going to let it slide for now, because when I get to that point, there was no coming back from it.

****

Today was the day of our date and I was excited as fuck.

I haven't been on a date since Malcolm and I broke up, and I was lowkey nervous. There was literally no reason for me to be nervous though, this was Durrell we're talking about.

"You look cute as fuck" Paris said to me. I smiled at her.

"Thanks bestie". She was here to watch the kids for me and was just as excited as I was.

"I'm ready for 7:30, but it's slow so I'm not complaining" I said taking a seat at my desk. I had two hours before I could clock out and time was dragging. Instead of working, I sat there scrolling through TikTok, talking to Paris and taking pictures. I was tempted to send a few selfies to Durrell but I didn't want him to see me until he got here.

Finally, it was 5 minutes before I could clock out. I had actually started to work so that the time would go by faster. I looked up from my laptop and noticed Durrell pulling into the driveway. A big smile appeared on my face. I glanced at the time and noticed I had 2 minutes before I could clock out. Saying fuck it, I went ahead and clocked out. Those two minutes wouldn't hurt me.

I opened the front door and stepped outside. His trunk was open and I saw his side profile rummaging through the trunk. When he heard the front door close, he looked up and our eyes locked. He smiled widely showing off his pearly whites.

"Got damn! You look gorgeous!" he said as I made my way over to him. I wrapped my arms around his neck and pecked his lips.

"Thank you, baby," I told him. I had on a black one shoulder jumpsuit with the sides cut out and some black sandals. I was going to wear heels, but I didn't want my feet to hurt. I washed my hair last night and made sure to flat iron it today so it was fresh. I also did a full face of make-up which I haven't done in forever, but tonight was special to me.

I took in his appearance. He had on a blue Nike shirt with

black shorts and black and white Nike dunks to match. Of course, he had on his signature cologne, his Cartier glasses, diamond stud earrings and a small chain. He looked so good I almost wanted to say fuck the date and take him upstairs, but I'd wait until later.

"You look good too" I told him.

"I know that" he joked. I playfully pushed him. "You ready? I'm hungry as hell". I nodded my head yes.

"Yeah, let me just go get my purse and let Paris know we're leaving".

"Bae, we taking your car. I don't know what you thought this was" he said with a slight chuckle.

"Why?"

"What you mean why? Yo shit better. Imma drive though". I laughed. He wasn't lying. My car was newer, so I had no complaints. I walked back into the house to grab my belongings and let everybody know I'd be back later.

Climbing into the passenger seat of my truck, I put my seat belt on and glanced over at Durrell who was adjusting the seat and mirrors.

"Yo short ass don't need to sit this damn close" he complained.

"Boy shut the fuck up. That's what's comfortable for me".

"Damn this shit so close. My eleven-year-old don't even need to sit this close up".

"I hate you" I stated playfully.

Once he got comfortable, he connected his phone to the Bluetooth, played some music and then pulled off. The car ride to the restaurant was nice. We didn't talk, but we didn't need to. We were too busy singing our hearts out to every song that played. I didn't know where he was taking me. I'd asked a few times but he told me to stop being nosy.

After about fifteen minutes of driving, we pulled up to Ruth Chris' Steakhouse. *Not he tryna impress me,* I thought to myself. He knew I loved steak so I appreciated the thought. Plus, I'd only been to Ruth Chris once in my adult life so it was fairly new to me. Walking inside, he let the hostess know he had a reservation and she assured us that our table would be ready in a few minutes.

"Oh, you made a reservation? Fancy" I joked.

"Got to. I didn't want to be waiting all day, and I know how you get when you're hungry. We ain't got time for that" he joked back.

We made small talk for a few minutes while we waited for our table. Finally, they came over and let us know we had an option of sitting in the main dining area or sitting in the lounge area where the bar was but the dining area seating would take a little longer. Not wanting to wait any longer, I chose to sit in the lounge area. They led us over to a table in the middle of the room. Once seated, the waiter came over, introduced himself and provided menus and water. I immediately grabbed the menu so that I could figure out what I wanted to eat. After a few moments, I felt a pair of eyes on me. I looked up and saw Durrell staring.

"What?" I asked.

"You are beautiful". I couldn't stop the smile from forming.

"Thank you, baby".

"I hate that I'm so far from you. I'm about to come over there" he said getting up. He looked around and found a chair nearby and scooted it over next to me.

"You're so cute".

"That was way too far. I'm tryna be all up on you" he said and I giggled. The waiter came back to take our order and then left again.

We sat and talked and sipped our drinks, waiting for our food to come out. I was thoroughly enjoying his company.

Everything just flowed so naturally with us. Nothing was ever forced.

"You know this is our first date ever, right?" he told me. I looked at him with my eyebrows scrunched together trying to remember.

"Are you sure?"

"Yeah, we've never been on a date before".

"That's cap. We went to the movies when we were younger".

"That was with other people, I'm talking about just me and you". I thought about it for a moment.

"Oh damn, you right. That's crazy".

"Ain't it. I can't believe we on a date." he said and we laughed simultaneously.

The food came and he went back to his spot across the table from me. We continued to talk and laugh while we ate. Everything was literally perfect. When we were done eating, he paid the tab and we walked out hand in hand.

"I'm lowkey full". I told him once we were in the car. That big ass steak and mac n cheese hit the spot.

"Damn I guess you don't want movie popcorn huh?"

"What you mean?"

"We were about to go to the movies but if you full and you wanna go home we can do that" he said smirking at me.

"You know damn well I love the movies and movie popcorn, stop playing with me" I said smiling.

"That's what I thought, greedy ass girl" he said pulling off. I stared at him for a few minutes. The man was so damn fine to me. Watching him drive turned me on in a way that I couldn't explain. I can't wait until we get back to the house.

Durrell

Autumn insisted that I stop at the store to get other snacks before we went to the movies. For somebody that was full off of the food we just ate at the restaurant, she was being greedy as fuck. I didn't care though; she can get whatever she wanted from me.

I'm not sure what I expected from tonight, but this was way better than anything I could have made up in my head. Shit was so easy with Autumn, in every aspect. She genuinely fucked with me and I really appreciated that. Her ass could tell when it was something bothering me without me saying a word and then get me to actually talk about it and we come up with a solution. The girl was hands down my best friend. No arguing, no nagging, no questioning my true intentions. This is all every man ever wanted, but yet, I hadn't completely stopped fucking with Rochelle. I know I needed to, but cutting those ties with your baby mom's is hard as hell.

Since it was so late, the regular theaters were closed so we decided to go to the drive in. Once we got there, I paid the admission fee, found our screen, parked and then went to get snacks. As I stood in the concessions line, my phone started to vibrate. I pulled it out of my pocket and saw that Rochelle was calling. I took a deep breath before answering.

"Yeah?"

"Where the fuck have you been all day?"

"Working earlier, out now" I said dryly. "Why?"

"Nigga because I texted you. I need you to sit with the kids tonight, I got called in for an extra shift" she said. I ran my hands down my face. This couldn't be a worse time.

"I'm busy right now. You can't ask your mom?"

"Busy doing what? With your bitch ass friends? Nigga, I don't give a fuck. Come sit with your fucking kids. They're sleeping anyway!" she fussed.

I pulled the phone away from my face and looked at the time. The movie was about to start and I wasn't cutting this date any shorter than I had to. Especially since this was something last minute.

"Alright. I'll be there. Give me a few hours".

"That's cool. I don't have to be there until one".

"What time you getting off?"

"I think 7".

"Alright" I said and disconnected the call.

Sighing, I shoved my phone back in my pocket. I really wasn't trying to leave Autumn tonight. I was tryna lay-up with her after the movie, but duty calls. She was gonna be mad as hell that I had to leave her and she'd probably start thinking a bunch of crazy shit. *Damn, Imma have to make up something.*

I bought the snacks and headed back to the car, the entire time trying to come up with what I would tell her once we got back to her house. I still had nothing by the time I reached the car. I handed the popcorn to Autumn and her eyes lit up.

"Thank you" she said smiling.

"You really greedy, you know that right?"

"I don't care" she said popping a kernel in her mouth and smacking unnecessarily.

I chuckled and shook my head climbing into the trunk next to her. We let down her back seats so that we could stretch out and watch the movie. After the previews, the movie started. Every few minutes, I'd look over at her. She was deep into the movie, but she also looked happy and at peace. I smiled slightly watching her devour the popcorn.

She must have felt me staring at her because she looked over at me and gave me a small smile. Against my will, my dick jumped. I'm sick I had to leave her after this, when all I really wanted to do was eat her pussy and make her feel good.

Once she was done with her popcorn, she scooted over next to me and cuddled up to me, pressing her ass on my pelvis. Again, my dick jumped.

"That's how you feel?" she whispered.

"That's how you got me feeling" I said kissing her cheek. I wrapped my arms around her waist and we continued to watch the movie. If it wasn't so many people around, I'd take her down through there right now, but I was trying to be respectful.

We talked shit about the movie periodically, laughing at how dumb some of the characters were. Once the movie was over, we pulled the seats back up, got in the front and pulled off. As I was driving, I grabbed her hand and brought it to my lips. The ride back to her house was about twenty minutes. We rode in comfortable silence, listening to the music. She was lost in her thoughts and I was lost in mine. Mainly, I was trying to figure out what I was going to say when she realized I wasn't coming in with her.

I pulled into her driveway and turned the ignition off. We both got out and she grabbed her leftover food from the passenger's side. She fumbled with her keys at the side door before unlocking it and opening the door.

"Did you have fun love birds?" her best friend Paris asked as we made our way into the living room.

"We had a great time" Autumn beamed. Paris smiled at her.

"I'm glad you had fun bestie".

"How were the kids?"

"Angels" she said and they both giggled. "Armon fussed a little when I laid him down, but other than that everything was fine. I ate, watched some TV, took a nap. You need to be gone more often" she said to her. Autumn playfully sucked her teeth.

"Don't worry, she will be" I chimed in. They both gave each other a look.

"I know that's right bae" Autumn said kissing me. She slipped her tongue in my mouth and instantly I knew what type of time she was on.

"Alright, that's my que. Nasty asses" Paris said getting off the couch and grabbing her belongings. Autumn went into the kitchen to put her leftovers away.

"I'm about to head out too baby" I said following her since the side door was right next to the kitchen. Autumn whipped her head in my direction with a confused expression plastered on her face.

"What? You're not staying?" she asked with her lip poked out. She was so cute when she was being a spoiled brat. For a second, I thought about saying fuck Rochelle and her job, but if I did that, I'd never hear the end of it.

"Not tonight baby. I gotta go handle something" I told her in the best way I could without lying. That answer didn't seem to work for Autumn because she poked her lips out even further.

"It can't wait? I wanted to lay up with you" she said walking towards me. "And I wanted to say hi to my bestie" she said grabbing my manhood through my shorts.

"Girl, stop playing" I said taking a slight step back. I stuck my lips out for a kiss and she obliged. We kissed for a few moments before I pulled away. "No sex on the first date" I told her and she giggled.

"Boy we've been having sex for months, tonight ain't no

different".

"Tonight is different. It's our first date and I said no sex on the first date. I'll be back tomorrow to get you right" I said gripping her ass. She sighed and pouted but agreed.

"Fine. Now you wanna be all respectful and shit" she joked.

"Actually, that first time was your fault. You seduced me, talking all that spin the block shit" I told her as I recalled the first time we had sex since reconnecting. "Actually, the very first time was your fault too my baby. You just a freaky little girl" I said and she gave me the middle finger.

"Get out of my face before I fuck you right now" she challenged. For the third time that night, my dick jumped. If only she knew there was nothing that I wanted more than for her to sit on this dick. Before I gave in to temptation, I decided to leave. I gave her a quick peck and then told her I'd see her tomorrow.

Driving to Rochelle's house, I was pissed. She never called me for this type of shit so I know she really didn't have anybody else to sit at her house. It was always somebody there. If it wasn't her mama or brother, it was her friends. Pretty ironic how tonight was the night that no one was around.

I wasn't against spending time with my kids at all or even looking out for Rochelle when she needed it, the timing was just fucked up.

"Wassup" I greeted as I walked through the front door.

"Damn, finally" she complained moving around the living room collecting her belongings.

I sucked my teeth and plopped down on the couch, grabbing the remote in the process. Without so much as a thank you or goodbye, she walked out of the house, slamming the door. That's the shit that pissed me off, but it was typical Rochelle. She had such a sense of entitlement sometimes. I chilled on the couch, scrolling through social media, laughing at the wild posts people shared on Facebook.

I didn't even realize I dozed off until I heard the faint sound of my son crying in his room. Looking around, I saw that it was daylight. I grabbed my phone to check the time, but my phone was dead. Stretching, I got up from the couch and went to tend to my boys; changing diapers, brushing teeth and making them some cereal and a bottle for breakfast. After they were situated and playing in the living room, I went to get myself together. By the time I got out of the shower, Rochelle was back.

"How were they last night?" she asked stripping out of her work clothes. I took the opportunity to scan over her body. After two kids, she still looked good. She was lighter than Autumn with light caramel skin, full lips, big breasts and a nice pair of thighs. She had a decent amount of ass too, but she wasn't fucking with Autumn in that department. For a moment, my mind shifted to Autumn. I was still mad that I didn't get a chance to lay up with her last night, but I would definitely be popping up over there later today.

"Durrell" Rochelle called out.

"Huh?"

"I asked how were they last night?" Rochelle repeated.

"Oh, they were cool. You know the lil homies never give me problems like they do you". She waved me off.

"Well, thank you. I didn't mean to interrupt whatever was so important yesterday" she said in a shady tone. Instead of responding, I continued to get myself together for the day. "Where are you about to go?" she asked once she noticed that I grabbed my keys.

"I got a few moves to make". I never told her my whereabouts. The less she knew, the better.

"Are you coming back later? I'm probably cooking before my shift tonight".

"Probably not, but still put up a plate for me" I told her and kissed the side of her face.

I sat with my boys for a few minutes before heading out. I needed to speak to my lawyer about my settlement check. A couple years back, I was in an Uber and the driver got into a pretty bad accident. I was hurt, but nothing too serious. My grandma encouraged me to take some legal action, and I recently received word that since the driver was at fault Uber would be issuing a settlement check to avoid any further action or court cases.

I also needed to go to the studio at some point today. At 28 years old, I was an up and coming rapper in Detroit. Music had always been a passion of mine, I even recorded a few songs, but I never took it seriously until now. I realized that I'm too damn old to still be in the streets, and aside from hustling, this is the only thing I'm good at that I really love. Granted, I could easily go and get a 9 to 5, but that would be my absolute last resort. As long as I wasn't struggling and I could take care of myself and my kids, I would continue to do what worked for me regardless of what anybody said.

This rap thing was going pretty well, especially for me just starting out. I shot my first video a few months ago, uploaded it to YouTube a few days ago and already have 10,000 views. Rochelle hated that I was into music, but she fake supported to make me happy. She swore she really did support me in whatever I chose to do, but I wasn't stupid. I hardly heard her mouth about it now though. I guess she got used to it. As long as she and our kids were taken care of, she didn't have too many complaints. Well, she did, but financially, she didn't really have to worry about too much. Of course, she made her own money so she didn't need me, but it wasn't always like that.

Rochelle liked to act like I was the reason that our relationship was on again, off again, but that wasn't the case. She always failed to mention the fact that she was the one who initially stepped outside of our relationship. Granted, she didn't fuck another nigga, but she did have an emotional connection with someone else a few years back. To me, that was worse than just fucking the nigga. Women leave the relationship emotionally and mentally before they leave physically. Whenever she and I were into it or on a break, she'd go back and fuck with this nigga. I'm sure they fucked by now, but she'd never admit it.

After I found out about him, I began to do my thing. There had been countless arguments and not just with me and her. She'd argue with anybody she assumed was fucking around with me. Especially the ones that she felt like I actually liked and fucked with heavy. She even fought a few hoes, but she never left because she knew I took care of her ass. Yeah, she had jobs here and there, but the majority of the bills and everything was taken care of by me up until recently. While she may fuss and fight, she always came back, so I felt like I could always do what I want.

That's where she and Autumn differ. Autumn had gone through that phase with her baby daddy. She expressed to me how stupid she felt for staying around for so long, but I assured her she wasn't stupid. She was just in love. Plus, I knew the real her. Before she fell in love and endured all that bullshit with that lame ass nigga. Within the few months that we've been kicking it, I could tell she was getting back to the old her, the one that didn't take nobody's shit. You might be able to make a mistake once, but twice was definitely pushing it. Autumn would get the fuck on. That I knew for sure. That's part of the reason why I'd been hesitant to take shit to the next level with her. I loved her and I wanted to be with her, but I didn't want to end up hurting her. I wanted to do things the right way or she'd hate me forever.

Plus, I wasn't ready to really let go of Rochelle yet, considering everything that we'd been through. I couldn't pretend like there were no feelings there just because Autumn was in the picture. Rochelle got on my fucking nerves and yes Autumn was making me happy as hell, but I just didn't know how that was going to go trying to leave Rochelle completely alone. I was conflicted and I knew it was selfish as hell, but if I could have them both, why wouldn't I?

Autumn

It's been a couple of weeks since our date and things have been better than ever. It felt good to finally not be worried about anything. The only thing that I wish was a little better was this situation with my baby daddy, but that was minor. That bitch would just have to stay mad because my opinion isn't going to change, and really, it shouldn't matter. I was still a little pissed off about that slick ass comment that she made about my parenting, but I was doing my best to ignore it. I ended up having to block her on Facebook and Instagram because she kept DM'ing me trying to get a reaction. I'm trying my hardest to be the bigger person, but it was getting hard to do.

Malcolm was getting the kids a little later so I would have the weekend to myself. I planned for it to just be me, Durrell and this bed. I didn't want to do shit but eat, sleep, watch tv and fuck. I deserved it.

Durrell came to get the kids and no words were really spoken between the two of us. He grabbed their bags off of the hallway floor and walked away without so much as a hi. I shrugged it off. I could care less about that man's funky ass attitude. Had he not opened his mouth, pillow talking with his bitch there would be no issue. Well, maybe there would. Maybe homegirl just wanted a reason to go back and forth with me just because I'm his babies' mother. Either way, I couldn't make their issues my issues. I went back upstairs to finish getting ready. I was about to go out and get crab legs with my friends.

Once I was done getting dressed, I looked myself over in the mirror and began snapping pictures.

"You look good bae. Who the fuck you trying to look good for? Because I ain't gon be there" Durrell joked.

"My other nigga" I joked back.

"Yeah alright, get fucked up" he said walking up to me and grabbing me by my neck. I grinned. He knew I liked that. "You a freaky ass little girl".

"Who little?" I asked bringing my face closer to his.

"Girl you better stop playing" he said quickly pecking my lips and then releasing me. He got behind me, grabbed the phone and began taking a few pictures with me. Once we were done, he found the one he liked and set it as my wallpaper. "Yo other nigga gon' be mad as fuck when he sees your screensaver" he said handing the phone back to me.

"You are irritating" I giggled. I got a text message saying my friends were on their way, so I gathered my things to head out. "Are you staying here or you're leaving?" I asked, lowkey hoping he stayed.

"Imma leave out to grab some weed, but I'll be back" he said and I nodded my head. "I love you" he said kissing my lips.

My heart started beating rapidly. Is this real? What do I say? What do I do? I looked into his eyes, almost waiting for him to say sike or start laughing to let me know that this was a joke, but that never came. I saw nothing but sincerity in his face.

"You love me?"

"Damn, I guess I haven't said that out loud huh?" he said. By the expression on his face, it seemed that he was realizing what he just let slip out of his mouth.

"No, you haven't. What do you mean out loud? You've been thinking about it for a minute?"

"Hell yeah. Honestly, Autumn, I been loving your ass since I was 13, ok? I don't think that shit will ever go away. I thought it was gone since we both moved on and had other relationships, but these past few months, those same feelings have come back, but harder" he said looking in my eyes. "Everything is so easy with you. Even when you get on my nerves, you really ain't on my nerves and that's crazy as hell because people really be on my nerves" he said and we shared a laugh. "But for real, I love you, and I ain't afraid to say that shit to you or nobody else".

"I love you too" I said kissing his lips. Our kiss intensified as his hands found its way to my ass cheeks, squeezing them. A low, soft moan escaped my lips. "Baby, I gotta go" I said in between kisses. Instead of releasing me, he pushed me onto the bed. Before he could climb on top of me, I put my hand up. "For real" I said, my eyes pleading for him to stop. If he kept trying, I was going to give in, and I really wanted to go have dinner with my girls.

"You lucky I know you don't play about them nasty ass crab legs". He helped me up from the bed and slapped my ass.

"I'll be back to finish what you just started" I said grabbing his manhood through his basketball shorts and heading out of the room.

"Girl, see, doing shit like that ain't helping".

"Bye fool" I called out walking out of the door.

I made it to the restaurant in about fifteen minutes. Thankfully, they hadn't been seated yet. We made small talk until we were seated at our table and then immediately ordered drinks.

"What the hell you smiling so hard for? What did my cousin do?" Paris asked me.

"Huh?"

"Mmmhmm, over there glowing and shit. Yo nasty ass was sucking dick before you got here, wasn't you?" Shani asked and the girls joined in laughter.

"Girl, no, Imma do that when I leave here" I said with an evil grin.

"Ok, so why you over there all smiling and shit? What happened?" my best friend Layla asked me. Really, all these hoes were my best friends for different reasons. I'm glad that we were all able to hang out and it was never any animosity. Everybody got along.

"Durrell said he loved me before I left" I told them and held the menu over my face.

"What!?" they exclaimed in unison.

"Y'all it caught me so off guard. All I could do was stare at him".

"So, you didn't say you love him back? Because we all know you do" Raegan chimed in.   "Exactly" Layla said.

"I said it back" I admitted.

"Ole in love ass bitch. How the fuck you fall out of love with your baby daddy and then back in love with your first love" Paris joked. "I'm happy for you bestie, you deserve it. I told you somebody was going to come along and love you and my kids. You used to say 'I got too much baggage, what if this, what if that" she said mocking me. "Now look at you, in love". I couldn't help but giggle because she was right.

On more than a few occasions Malcolm would tell me that niggas would only fuck me and wouldn't want to really be with me, especially with two kids. I'm realizing that I actually started to believe that. I'm worthy of receiving genuine love from a man and my kids deserved to see their mom being loved correctly.

We continued to talk and joke, enjoying the drinks and eventually the food. The crab legs were bomb as always and I made sure to stuff myself because I wasn't taking any of this home.

Once I got home, I stripped out of my clothes, down to my panties and bra. Laying on my king size bed, I grabbed my phone and FaceTimed Durrell.

"Wassup baby" he answered. "Got damn you look good" he

complimented noticing I was half naked. I smirked slightly.

"Thank you, bae. Where you at?"

"At my people house right now. I'm about to go grab some weed and then I'll be there".

"Hurry up".

"Shit, I am. Look at what's waiting on me. Just unlock the door bae, I don't know if you gon be sleep or not". We hung up the phone and I laid around watching TV, eventually falling asleep.

I woke up to Armon screaming like he usually did. I don't understand why babies had to scream when they wake up. Like, just wake up, why are you mad? I hopped up, immediately going into Mommy mode. I woke MJ up to get everyone's teeth brushed and then went downstairs to get them something to eat. After they ate and MJ was situated with virtual school, I went back upstairs to get showered and dressed before work.

I grabbed my phone, about to connect it to my speaker in the bathroom, but all the notifications stopped me in my tracks. I looked around, suddenly remembering that Durrell never called me and never popped up last night like he was supposed to. I opened my phone and saw that I had no notifications from him, however, I had about 4 missed calls and 2 voicemails from an unknown number. I listened to each voicemail.

"Baby…" I heard Durrell say in a groggy voice. "Call me when you get a chance, it's an emergency". The next voicemail was also from him. "Answer the damn phone girl!" I chuckled slightly at his attempt to yell, but wondered why he sounded like that. He better have a good excuse for why he didn't come over last night. I dialed his number, but it went straight to voicemail. I started to send a text, but decided not to. Instead, I went ahead and turned my music on to take a shower.

Just as I was getting out of the shower, my phone started to ring. I noticed it was the same number Durrell called from.

"Hello?"

"Bae where the hell you been?!" Durrell asked in a raspy tone.

"I was sleep. Where the hell have you been and who's number is this?"

"I'm so sorry I didn't make it over there. I'm at the hospital".

"The hospital? For what?"

"I got shot baby". I pulled the phone away from my face, frowning.

"What you mean you got shot? Shot where? When? How? Why? Are you ok?" I fired off question after question.

"That hoe ass nigga shot me 3 times. Once in my hand, And twice in my leg. This shit hurt I ain't gon lie, and I lost a couple fingers".

"A couple of fingers?!" I yelled. My heart felt like it was in my ass. So many questions ran through my mind.

"Imma tell you the whole story when I get out, I don't even wanna talk about it right now for real. Some hoe ass shit. I just wanted you to know what was going on before you saw it on the internet. Are you ok? How was dinner?"

"How are you concerned about me and you're the one laid up in a damn hospital bed!?"

"Baby, calm down, I'll be straight. Talk to me. How was dinner?" he repeated. I gave him the run-down of last night and we talked for a while like nothing was wrong. "Oh, baby, they're about to take me to do some tests or something. Imma call you when I get back".

"Ok, I love you".

"I love you too girl. Don't watch none of our shows without me, Imma beat yo ass, eight fingers and all". I giggled.

"Bye fool". We hung up and I sat in disbelief. Who the fuck shot my man? I tapped on my phone screen and went to Facebook.

Coincidentally, the first thing I saw when I opened the app was Durrell's post letting everyone know he was shot but still alive. I noticed that he received over 200 likes and comments on the picture and I frowned. He ain't ever got this many reactions on a post and now all of a sudden, he's a celebrity. I scrolled through the compliments and rolled my eyes at every female that posted their condolences.

Scrolling through the likes, I saw a name that caught my attention. *Rochelle Harrington.* I knew that was his second baby mama's name. Unable to resist, I clicked on her name and her page popped up. She was a decent looking girl, but her chin bothered me. I barely had to scroll before a status caught my attention.

*Get well soon @Durrell Johnson, love you nigga *kissy emoji*.*

I expressed on more than a few occasions that I never wanted Durrell to lie to me. I always wanted him to be upfront and honest, because there was no reason to lie to me. All feelings aside, Durrell was my friend and if nobody else understood his ass, I did. I told him that I kind of felt a way about Rochelle simply because their youngest child was the same age as Armon, but he assured me when we first started talking that just as I had moved on from Malcolm, he had moved on from her. I had no reason to think otherwise, until now. I mean, the status wasn't enough to think that they were fucking around because if Malcolm was to get shot, I'd still be there, regardless of our current situation. At the end of the day, we had hella history and he was my family, but I don't know if I would've expressed an 'i love you' or a kissy emoji.

"I'm crazy. Why am I getting mad?" I asked myself aloud. Chuckling, I shrugged off my absurd thoughts and continued to get myself together.

Work dragged by. All I could think about was Durrell. I wanted to try and figure out what happened exactly, but I'd wait for him to tell me the story when he was ready. Right now, the only focus was him getting better.

Durrell

Hospital drugs were a hell of a thing. Once these mothafucka's started to wear off, you felt that shit for sure. I'm pissed that I'm laid up in this hospital bed instead of taking care of shit. Stupid mothafucka shot me over some goofy shit, but it was ok, because that nigga would see me again. I was going to wait until shit died down though. I may have been upset and wanting revenge, but I ain't no dummy. That nigga come up missing I'm the number one suspect.

"You ok?" Rochelle asked coming into the room. She'd been here since they first admitted me a few days ago. Actually, everybody had been up here. All my homies, my grandma, the rest of my family, my other baby mama. Everybody except Autumn. I'm kind of glad that Autumn hadn't been able to get up here though. I wanted to keep Rochelle and Autumn far away from each other for as long as possible.

"Yeah, I'm good. Just ready to go".

"They're supposed to be bringing your prescriptions and your discharge papers in the next couple of hours so you'll be out of here. Are you sure you want to recover at your grandma's? You know you're welcome at my house" she said and I gave her a slight smile.

"I appreciate the offer, but I know you have to work and deal with the boys. I'm gonna need around the clock care for a couple of weeks. You ain't gonna be able to do that on top of everything you already do. Don't worry, I'll be straight".

"Can't help but worry about your black ass now" she tried to make light of the situation. We sat around and talked for a while about nothing important, and then she got quiet.

"What are you over there thinking about?" she looked at me and gave me a blank stare. "What? What's on your mind?"

Instead of answering me, she dug in her purse and pulled out her phone. She tapped the screen for a few seconds and then walked over to the side of the bed, shoving the phone in my face.

"Who's this?" she asked. I looked at the screen, trying to figure out what I was looking at. Once I focused, I realized that it was a picture of me and Autumn posted on Autumn's story. It was a picture that we took last month. My face wasn't in it, but if you were fucking with me, you'd know it's me. There was no caption, just a few emojis indicating that she was praying for me and wishing me well. *Aww she posted me*, I thought to myself. It was taking everything in me not to smile. Just as I was about to answer her question, my grandmother and nurse walked in with my discharge papers. *Saved by the fucking bell.*

As Rochelle was helping me into the wheelchair to wheel me out of the hospital, my phone vibrated on the bed. I looked over at the screen to see who it was. *Sunshine* with the sunshine emoji and a blue heart appeared on the screen along with Autumn's gorgeous face. I glanced over at Rochelle. She was too busy talking to my nurse to be concerned with my phone. I quickly grabbed it off of the bed and sent Autumn a quick text.

Me: Getting discharged baby. Call you when I get home and settled.

*Sunshine: Ok *kissy face emoji**

Unbeknownst to Autumn, I gave her the nickname Sunshine because she was a fucking ray of sun in my dark ass life. I'd been through a lot in my life with my family, jail, relationships, and even though Autumn knew about a good chunk of it, she didn't know everything. Yet, she still managed to only see the good in me. Whenever I was around her, I felt at peace, happy. She always looked at me with those innocent eyes like I could do no wrong, which was funny because let my ex's, or even just my baby mamas tell it, everything I did was wrong.

Once I got home, or to my grandma's house I should say, my grandma made sure that I was as comfortable as I could be on this damn couch. I was kind of pissed that I had to sleep on a fucking couch after being shot the fuck up, but I didn't really have any other choice. I couldn't stay at my place because nobody would be there to take care of me 24/7.

"Are you comfortable grandbaby?" she asked.

My Grandma was my everything. She was more of a Mother to me than her daughter was. Not saying that I didn't love my Mama to death, because I did, but our relationship wasn't always the best. When we were younger, she was out in the streets a bit, so a lot of the love and support I should have received from her never came. That's where my Grandma stepped in. She was the sweetest and most loving little lady, but she also didn't take no shit. In a sense, she reminded me of Autumn, sweet as pie, but will still cuss you the fuck out and put you in your place if need be.

***

It's been about a week since I got shot and I could tell this road to recovery would be a long one. I was tired of changing bandages, walking with this dumb ass limp and not being able to really do shit for myself. I was sleep most of the day because of the pain meds and when I wasn't sleep, I was in pain and uncomfortable. I wanted to get the hell off of this couch and out of this house. I hated sitting in one spot for too long.

"Grandbaby, your phone is ringing" my Grandma, said taking me out of my thoughts. I looked at the screen and smiled, swiping to answer the incoming FaceTime call.

"Hey bae, how're you feeling?"

"Better now that I see your fine ass" I smiled. I haven't seen Autumn since the day I got shot and I had to admit, I missed the hell out of her. This is the longest we've gone without seeing each other since we started fucking around and I didn't like that shit.

"I miss you" she said in the cutest voice.

"I miss you too baby. I go to the doctor tomorrow, so hopefully they give me some good news. You still coming to see me?"

"Is the sky blue? Yeah, I'm coming. I'll be there right after I drop the kids off". She smiled at me causing me to smile. We talked for a few minutes before she told me she had to get back to work.

"That was Rochelle?" my Grandma, asked being nosy. I gave her a knowing look. She knew damn well that wasn't Rochelle.

"Nah Grandma, that wasn't Rochelle".

"Oh, you got a new girlfriend?"

"Grandma, Rochelle ain't been my girlfriend for a minute".

"Well, what do you call it?" she asked folding her arms.

"It's complicated". I really didn't know how to explain whatever it was Rochelle and I were doing currently.

"Mmmhmm. Well, who is this new girl?"

"You'll meet her tomorrow" I told her. Thankfully, she dropped the subject and focused her attention on the TV in front of us.

***

The next day couldn't get here soon enough. The doctor told me that my two fingers were healing fine, but they were worried about the way my fourth finger was healing. They had to cut the tip of my index and middle finger on my right hand and they were now debating the fourth. When they took the bandage off for examination, it fucked me up. I can't lie, I shed a few tears. I never imagined that I'd be crippled or have a disability. Especially not in this way. After we left the doctor, I was fucked up and didn't really wanna talk to anybody, but leave it to Autumn to give me a pep talk and get me back right. That girl was something else and she didn't even know it.

I was currently sitting in the living room along with my little sister and brother, waiting on Autumn. Well, they were watching Power, I was waiting on my baby. As if on cue, my phone vibrated. I hurriedly answered.

"You outside?"

"Dang, you miss me for real huh?"

"You have no idea".

"No, I'm not outside yet. I just dropped off the kids, so I'm on my way". The thought of her on her way to me forced a smile on my face.

"Ok, you got my location, right?"

"Yes baby, I'll be there in 12 minutes" she said giggling.

"Alright, let me know when you're outside". Once we hung up, I scrolled through social media to pass the time.

Sunshine: Outside

"Aye, can one of y'all go open the door for Autumn?"

"Who is Autumn?" my sister asked.

"My girl" I told her. She didn't say anything, just got up and did what I asked. My little sister was also my baby. Actually, all the women in my family had me wrapped around their little fingers. Anything they asked for, they could get from me and they knew that shit.

"Hey" I heard my sister say. "You can go right up the stairs".

"Hey, how're you doing". The sound of my baby's voice made my heart swell. I felt like a 13-year-old all over again. I heard footsteps and then my baby appeared in the doorway. "Hey everybody" she said sweetly. I took in her appearance. She was wearing a blue two-piece set that hugged her body perfectly along with some UGGS. The outfit was simple, yet she made that shit look good as hell. When her eyes landed on me, her smile brightened.

"Take your shoes off" I told her.

I watched as she removed her shoes and placed her jacket and purse on a chair close to her. She walked over to me and took a seat next to me on the couch. I wrapped my arm around her pulled her close and inhaled her scent. Damn I missed the way she smelled; cocoa butter mixed with some fruity shit. I couldn't put my finger on it. Kind of reminded me of candy. Either way, she smelled amazing and I was mad as hell I couldn't sneak off and eat her alive.

"How are you feeling?" concern dripping from her tone. Looking at her eyes, I could see the worry, which I thought was adorable.

"Calm down. I'm fine. Better than I was earlier. Way better now that you're here. I missed you" I admitted.

"I missed you too. You have no idea".

"Aye bro, this the same Autumn from back in the day?" my brother Messiah asked. I nodded my head yeah. "Hell naw, that's crazy".

"I know that's not baby Messiah!?" Autumn screeched realizing who was sitting on the other side of the L-shaped couch. "Damn, how old are you now? Last time I saw you, you were like four or five years old".

"I'm nineteen now".

"Damn, we old as hell" Autumn said.

"Who is we? You the one that's 30" I joked, knowing she hated when I said that.

"Who's 30? Stop playing with me" she said cutting her eyes at me. I laughed in amusement. The three of us continue to talk in between watching the latest episode of Power. After a few minutes, my Grandma came into the room.

"Why are y'all so loud in here?" she asked ready to cuss one or all of us out. Her eyes landed on Autumn who looked a little nervous. "I'm sorry baby. How're you doing?"

"I'm good, how are you?"

"Doing good, I can't complain".

"Grandma, this is Autumn, Autumn, this is my Grandma". My grandma walked over and had Autumn stand up, pulling her in for a hug. I couldn't help but get a good look at Autumn's round ass as she hugged my Grandma. If I didn't know her personally, I'd swear she had ass shots or something. I mean, her shit didn't look super fake, but it definitely was huge to be a natural ass.

"You look familiar. Have we met before?"

Autumn frowned in confusion.

"I don't think we have. Have we?" she asked looking at me.

"I think y'all did meet once way back in the day but it was brief".

"Oh, y'all grew up together?" she asked taking a seat next to Messiah on the couch. We both ran down the story of how we met through Isaiah.

"This is the first girl I got pregnant, remember that?" I said trying to jog my Grandma's memory.

"Now why would you say that?" Autumn snapped.

"What? It's true" I shrugged.

"Oh yes, I remember now". I knew Autumn was embarrassed about that, but shit, it was a part of our history.

When I was 14 and Autumn was 15, she wound up pregnant. Both of our parents were pissed the fuck off, but nobody worse than Autumn's Mom. She was adamant about Autumn not being ready to take care of a baby and that she'd be having an abortion. My people always have and always will feel a way about abortions so they weren't feeling that shit at all. However, since

Autumn was a minor, we didn't really have any say in the matter and Autumn ended up having an abortion. Quiet as it's kept, I was happy that she forced Autumn into that abortion. We were just kids ourselves. We weren't ready to raise a baby.

I knew Autumn felt a way about it for a while, but eventually she realized it was for the best. We even had a running joke that if she was to get pregnant right now, we'd go to that same abortion clinic. She liked to say that I had enough kids for the both of us, and she wasn't entirely wrong.

A little while after Autumn had the abortion, we ended up breaking up because I started messing with my first baby mama, Ke'Asia. Shortly after we broke up, Ke'Asia popped up pregnant with our first child. That shit crushed Autumn, but oddly enough, we still fucked around a little bit up until I went to jail for the first time.

I called her a couple of times from jail and we were still friendly, but I remember that last time I called and I never called her again. That was the day she told me she had a boyfriend that she loved and he wouldn't appreciate us talking for real. Even back then, Autumn had that same loyalty about her that I loved. I couldn't do shit but respect it, but it did hurt a nigga a little bit. Still, I let her go and live her life with that nigga. We would talk periodically throughout the years and I knew they'd go through normal couple shit, but in recent years, I figured they were happy and married. I was clearly wrong.

"What are you over there thinking about?" Autumn asked interrupting my trip down memory lane.

"You" I said allowing her to rest her head on my chest. We sat around talking, laughing and watching TV. After a few hours, my Grandma went to her room, and my siblings left to be with their significant others, so it was just me and Autumn in the living room. I looked at the clock on my phone and saw that it was 2am. Looking down, Autumn's head was comfortably in my lap.

"Bae" I said shaking her lightly.

"Hmm?" she responded, damn near moaning. My dick jumped which caught me a little off guard, because for a minute I thought my shit was broke. I haven't gotten an erection since I got shot, so I was happy to know I could still fuck.

"Bae, wake up. It's late".

"What time is it?" she asked in a groggy voice.

"Almost 2". That caused her to sit up.

"Damn, for real? Time went by fast. I gotta get home" she said yawning and stretching.

"I hate that you're about to be out there driving by yourself. I wish I could come with you".

"I do too. But it's ok. Wait until your next doctor's appointment and if they give you the ok, I'll take care of you that weekend. Think of it as your Sweetest Day gift" she said offering a warm smile. I never celebrated Sweetest Day. To me, it was a made-up ass Midwest holiday, but females ate that shit up, so I'd oblige for her. Forcing myself up, I grabbed the cane the hospital issued me and walked her to the door.

"I'm happy you're still here" she said turning to face me.

"Me too baby, me too". She kissed my lips, pecking them at first. I grabbed her waist and pulled her into me, deepening the kiss.

"Alright now, you can't finish shit so don't start it" she said breaking away.

"I think I can" I said with an evil grin.

"Boy, bye" she laughed waving me off. "I'll text you when I get home" she said walking towards her car.

"I love you".

"I love you more".

It's been a few weeks since Durrell was shot, and this weekend was dedicated to my baby and making sure he was comfortable. He'd expressed on more than one occasion how he was uncomfortable on that couch and wanted to stretch out in the bed. He'd been doing great with recovery. He was moving around without his cane which was amazing. Still a little slow, but it was progress. The situation with his finger was still up in the air, but I was hopeful.

Shit with me had been smooth besides Malcolm. His Gemini had been Gemining lately. I never knew what personality I was going to get. When he wasn't around his girlfriend, he was cool, but I could always tell when she was close by. He'd start acting like an asshole. I tried not to give any energy to that situation though. To me, it was petty. Home girl had no reason not to like me. The petty side of me wanted to make it worse though. Since she already didn't like me, I wanted her to hate me. I unblocked her after a while just because. I knew she was watching my social media either from her page or a fake page, so I'd purposely share posts on Facebook about baby daddies or if a memory of Malcolm and I popped up, I posted it just to get under her skin. The way I see it, if you don't like me, you might as well take it up a notch and hate me.

"Mommy, can I live with my Daddy?" MJ asked out of nowhere.

"You want to live with your Daddy?" I repeated as if I hadn't heard him clearly. He shook his head yes. "Why?" I questioned. He shrugged his shoulders.

"Daddy lets me stay up and play the game". I looked at my oldest soon and shook my head.

"Boy, get out of my face" I said playfully.

"What? I'm just saying!" he said holding up his hands. My baby was named Malcolm junior for a reason. Sometimes his Dad, just jumped out of him, and each time it caught me off guard.

"I love that you love being with your Dad, baby. But no, you cannot live with him. Matter of fact, I take that back. You can ask him if you can live with him when you're with him this weekend, ok?"

"Ok! Are you going to see Rell?" he asked.

"Yes, why?"

"Can you tell him I said wassup and I hope he feels better". I looked up at him and smiled.

I loved the bond that Durrell was forming with my kids. Armon loved him, but then again, Armon loves everybody that shows him any kind of attention. Since MJ was older, it took a second to warm up to him, but they got along great. Really, all it took was for Durrell to go in MJ's room and play a few games of 2K. Now, they were besties and it was slightly annoying, but super cute.

"Yes, I will tell him baby" I assured him.

"Ok!" he said happily and then ran off to do whatever it was he was doing before. I got the kids prepared to go with Malcolm and waited for him to pick them up. Once they were gone, I called Durrell to let him know that I was on the way.

Me: Outside

Bae: Here I come

As I sat there waiting for Malcolm to come to the car, I scrolled through my social media, sharing a few funny posts on

Facebook.

"Boo!" Malcolm said snatching the car door open. I jumped.

"Stop playing so much! Damn. You scared me!"

"You shoulda been paying attention instead of on that phone". I waved him off. He climbed in the car and kissed my cheek. "What you got planned for me this weekend? You gon rub my feet?" he asked putting his foot on my dashboard, knowing I hated that shit. I cut my eyes at him and he immediately put his foot down.

"Now you know damn well I'm not rubbing your stinky feet, don't do that".

"Girl, my shit smells good".

"I don't care what it smells like, I don't do feet". I twisted my face up in disgust. One thing I could stand was somebody's feet, especially men. They made my stomach turn. "I don't have anything planned. We're just going to chill like we were supposed to do the day you got shot" I said. I noticed him nodding his head in approval.

"I'm good with that. I'm just happy to be out of that damn house, I tell you that".

"I tell you that" I said mocking him. "You sound like an old ass man" I laughed.

"That was funny?" he said fake mad. He tried to keep a straight face, but then joined me in laughter. "Aww damn bae, I forgot my meds". I smacked my lips. "It's cool, we can just come back and grab them tomorrow".

"What? That doesn't even make sense. I'm still close, I can just turn around and grab them".

"Nah, it's cool. I just took some before I left, I'll be straight until the morning". I glanced over at him.

"Fuck what you talking about, I'm going to get them" I said putting my turn signal on and switching lanes so that I could get off at the next exit.

"Nah, it's cool for real. I promise".

"Listen, if you start hurting Imma fuck you up".

"I believe you" he chuckled.

Once we made it home, I helped him out of the car, but he insisted he didn't need me to so I let him do his thing. Going up the stairs was a slight struggle, but we made it to my bedroom.

"Ooh it smells so damn good in here. I miss this smell" he said sniffing the air like a dog.

"You're dramatic" I laughed. "Oh, MJ said wassup and he hopes you feel better" I told him remembering what my baby asked me to say.

"He did for real?" he beamed. I shook my head. "Aww that's wassup. Lil homie love me. I fuck with that kid".

"The feelings are mutual". I watched as he removed his clothing before laying down. He knew I didn't play laying on my bed with outside clothes on. I put on a movie for us to watch and cuddled up with him. It had been almost a month since I had some alone time with him like this. I knew I missed this but I didn't realize how much until he was here with me.

I got so wrapped up in the movie that I forgot I had a gift for him. Checking the time, I saw that it was past midnight, which officially made it Sweetest Day. I hopped up from the bed with my phone in my hand.

"Where you going?"

"Bathroom" I lied.

I went into MJ's room and grabbed the gift bag that I hid in his closet. I placed the gift bag behind my back and made my way back to my room. Before opening the door, I made sure I turned the camera on so that I record the moment. Entering the room, Durrell's eyes immediately fell on me. He looked at me as if he knew I had something up my sleeve.

"Happy Sweetest Day!" I shouted pulling the gift bag from behind my bag.

"Girl, you are something else. I told yo ass I didn't want anything, I just wanted to be with you" he reminded me. He told me constantly over the last couple of weeks that he didn't really fuck with this holiday and that he didn't want anything, but since when do I listen to him?

"Since when do I listen to you?" I said voicing my thought aloud. He shook his head and smiled taking the bag from my hand. He pulled out the card and placed it next to him before digging in the bag for the gift. I slapped his hand.

"Ahh, what hell? What I do?" he whined sounding like a little boy.

"Read the card first!" Sucking his teeth, he did as I asked. "You not gon read it out loud?"

"Girl, you know what it says!" he argued.

"Bae" I whined. He looked at me and I pouted, poking my lip out.

"Alright, let me read what you wrote" he said clearing his throat. "I know you said you didn't want anything, but fuck you" he said chuckling at my message. He flipped me the bird before continuing to read. "It's nothing big, just a little token to show you that I love you and I appreciate you. Thank you for swooping into my life at a time I least expected it, but needed the most. I've been the happiest I've ever been and a lot of that is because of you. Thank you for doing nothing but being amazing to me. I love you the most" he read quietly. When he was done, he stayed silent, avoiding eye contact with me.

"Are you ok?" I asked, starting to worry.

"I'm good. You're just...amazing as fuck. You know that, right?" he asked looking me in my eyes.

"Duh, I been tryna tell you that my whole life" I joked.

"You always gotta ruin the moment" he laughed.

"I didn't ruin it, I made it lighter. You tryna get all sappy and deep. I know how you feel about me".

"Do you, really?"

"And do" I stated. "Go ahead, open the bag", I said granting him permission.

He dug in the bag and pulled out the cologne that I'd purchased. I watched as he looked at me with a smile then looked back at the cologne. He took the top off and smelled it.

"Yeah, you know me fasho. This smells good as fuck".

"You like it?"

"Hell yeah".

"Good! I smelled it at the mall and I'm like yeah, this smells just like something he'd wear. Aww yay me I did good".

"You did bae, you did".

"It's something else in there" I told him.

"Well, I see that. This big ass bag". He dug further in the bag and pulled out a black Nike tech fit. "I thought you were buying this for MJ? You a sneaky mothafucka" he said holding the hoodie up to his body. A week ago, I texted him some pictures of the tech fit in different colors asking which one he liked the most. He picked black or blue. I tried to get blue since it was our favorite color, but they didn't have his size, so I ordered black instead.

"Actually, I didn't say that. You just assumed it was for MJ and I didn't deny it" I shrugged.

"I love it baby, thank you. Can't believe you did this shit. Damn" he said under his breath.

"You're welcome. Nothing major" I said taking the bag and putting it on the floor.

"Come here" he said and I scooted closer to him. "No, I mean, here" he said patting his lap.

"I don't want you to start hurting".

"Girl, don't worry about me. Climb yo ass up here". Without a second thought, I sat up and straddled him. I noticed him wince and smacked my lips.

"See, nah".

"Chill out, I'm good".

"You sure?"

"Positive" he said making his dick jump. I looked down at his bulge that was directly under my center. He made his dick jump again. Looking up at me, he had a lazy grin on his face and I already knew where his mind was.

"That's how you feel?"

"That's how I been feeling baby".

I could tell that he was trying to fuck his way through the pain, but I chose not to say anything. Instead we went to sleep. I was sleeping good as hell until he shook me awake.

"Baby...baby we gotta go".

"Huh? What's wrong?"

"I tried to wait until the morning, but this shit is hurting. I need my meds". I smacked my lips. I wanted to smack him upside the head, but he was already in enough pain.

"I told yo ass that we should've went back and got them! Are you ok to walk down the steps by yourself?"

"Yeah, just give me a minute. I can do it" he said.

I watched as he struggled to get down the steps, but I didn't say anything. I just stood back and let him do what he needed to do. We got in the car and pulled off. The entire ride, he was doubled over in pain. I hated seeing him like that.

I sped to his grandma's house, not caring about red lights or the police. About 5 minutes later, I pulled up in front of her house and parked.

"Are you going to be ok?"

"Yeah baby. Imma take my meds, get a few hours of sleep and then you can come back and get me if I don't get dropped off".

"Ok" I nodded. I watched as he slowly got out of the car and walked to the front door. I waited until he was inside to pull off. One day, he was going to listen to me. I had some words for him, but I was going to let him get his rest for now.

<h1 style="text-align:center">Malcolm</h1>

"What time are we leaving?" Bianca asked from the bathroom.

We were about to go over my Pop's house and chill with my people for a while. They'd met Bianca a couple of times, and while they didn't have any problems with her, I knew it would take them some getting used to. For the past ten years, it's only been Autumn, so the change was a little weird for everyone involved, including me. I first introduced everyone to Bianca on my birthday/father's day weekend a few months ago. I could tell that everybody was confused wondering where Autumn was. We hadn't really told anyone that we broke up, we just did that shit, so I understood the confusion. However, they would rock with whatever I was with.

"I'm waiting on you slow poke" I teased.

She waved me off and continued primping in the mirror. I took that time to send a couple text messages. Halloween was in a couple of days and I was excited to take my boys trick or treating. This would be their first major holiday without both of us present, and I wanted the transition to be as smooth as possible. Armon was too young to know what was going on, but MJ wasn't. He knew his parents weren't together anymore and he knew we were both seeing other people, but I know it had to be a little weird for him, even if he didn't speak on it.

Finally, Bianca was ready to go. Once we made it to my Pop's crib, we greeted everyone and then settled in the living room, chopping it up and drinking. Before I knew it a few hours passed and the only ones left in the living room were me, Bianca, my brother Maurice, my sister Shay and my cousin Destiny. At this point, we were all a little tipsy, but Bianca was definitely drunk. I could always tell because she would start talking too much and getting belligerent.

"You talked to my sister lately?" Shay asked me. I gave her a look trying to signal that now wasn't the time to bring up Autumn, but she didn't get the hint. "What? I'm just curious. I haven't seen her in a while" Shay continued.

"Why you keep asking about her like I'm not right here?" Bianca asked. Shay frowned.

"What do you mean? This is my first time asking about the girl since we've been sitting here. It was just a question, calm down".

"Nah, y'all been making little smart remarks about his ex all night like I don't know who the fuck that is. Y'all miss her or something? You wanna be with her?" Bianca said getting louder with each word.

"B, chill. You getting loud" I said trying to diffuse the situation before it got heated. If I knew my family the way I think I did, this could go left really quick. Plus, everyone had been drinking and I knew how my sister and cousin got off the liquor.

"I'm not trying to get loud, I'm just saying" she said never taking her eyes off Shay.

"Girl, you trippin" she laughed waving her off. I looked over at Maurice who sat silently shaking his head. My brother was real laid back. He'd never insert himself in some bullshit unless it was absolutely necessary.

After a few minutes of silence, Destiny changed the subject and shifted the energy, thankfully. We all began to talk and laugh again.

"Shay, you don't like me?" Bianca blurted out, words slightly slurred.

"Huh?"

"I'm just saying. You brought that bitch up for nothing, disrespecting me like I'm not right here". I rubbed my hand across my face.

"Hold on, chill out. What you ain't gon do is disrespect that girl when she's not even here to defend herself" Destiny chimed in.

"I wasn't fucking talking to you. I was talking to Shay".

"And bitch I'm talking to you! You doing too much!" Destiny said raising her voice.

"I'm doing too much!? You don't see how that shit was disrespectful as fuck".

"Girl, I can ask about my fucking sister regardless of who the fuck is around" Shay stated in an irritated tone. Bianca chuckled.

"That's the thing. That's not your sister. Y'all not related. This" Bianca said pointing at me, "is your brother".

"And? Your point? She been around for ten plus years, that's family, flat out. You don't like her or something? Because you seem very bothered at just a slight mention of her. I'm trying to figure out what's the reason" Destiny said in a calmer tone than before.

"It's not that I don't like her, I just think she's a bitter baby mama" Bianca shrugged. I looked at her, surprised. This was news to me. I never heard her say that in regards to Autumn.

"Bitter how? Doesn't she have a whole new nigga?" Shay asked me. I nodded my head.

"Can we stop talking about this girl? She ain't even here bro" I said trying to change the subject.

"Her having a new nigga doesn't matter. When I met her over FaceTime, she definitely had an attitude. Then she went back and told my nigga he can do better and that I'm ugly. That doesn't sound like a bitter hating ass bitch to you?" she asked, ignoring my statement, waiting for them to answer.

"That doesn't even sound like Autumn. Malcolm, what happened?" Shay asked. Realizing that they weren't going to let this go, I ran down the entire situation. I explained that Autumn did reveal that she was working and irritated with a customer at the time which is why it looked like she had an attitude, but it wasn't directed towards us.

"There you go defending her" Bianca said getting upset with me.

"I'm not defending her bae; I'm just explaining what happened".

"Yeah, whatever".

"Ok, so if she said she was irritated because of work, why are you still thinking it's about you?" Shay asked trying to understand.

"Because why would you go back and tell this man he can do better and that I'm ugly? Like really? Ugly? I'm far from it baby. That's just some hating ass shit to me. Like girl if you want your baby daddy just let me know, I'll back off and y'all can be a happy family" she said scooting away from me.

"Man, chill out, she doesn't want me and I don't want her".

"Let me call her so we can get her side" Destiny said pulling out her phone.

"Nah, that ain't even necessary. I know what it is" Bianca said. Destiny and Shay looked at each other before laughing.

"Ok Bianca" Shay said. "Come on Des, we're about to go". I breathed a sigh of relief, thankful that this conversation was finally coming to an end.

"I'm about to get up out of here too bro" Maurice said standing up. He'd been so quiet, I damn near forgot he was in the room.

"Yeah, we're about to leave too. They asses done went to sleep on us" I chuckled referring to my Pop's and his wife.

My parents were no longer together. My Mom died when I was 16 of cancer. Shortly after that, my Pop's introduced us to his new woman, LaTisha. Even back then, I wasn't stupid. I'd seen her a few times when my mom was still alive and knew what was going on behind her back. I carried a lot of hate and resent me towards my Pops about that shit, but I never spoke on it in order to keep peace within the family. Plus, I felt like it wasn't worth it. My opinion and the way I felt about certain shit didn't really matter and wouldn't change anything, so I kept quiet.

We all walked out of the house, feeling the cool fall air immediately. I heard Destiny and Shay giggling while walking to their car and I led Bianca to my car. Before I could get to the passenger door and open it for her, she snatched away from me.

"What was said?" she yelled walking towards Destiny and Shay.

"What the fuck are you doing bro?" I asked walking behind her.

"These bitches got a lot of mouth now that we ain't in the same room. Talk yo shit louder. Don't be scary". I frowned in confusion. What the fuck was this girl talking about?

"I said you a weird ass obsessed ass bitch!" Destiny yelled. *Fuck.*

"*Oh* yeah? Talk that shit in my face bitch!" Bianca yelled back. I caught up to her and grabbed her arm pulling her back.

"Chill the fuck out!" I shouted.

"Let me fucking go Malcolm! Come talk that shit hoe! I'm right here!"

"Bitch you think I won't?!"

"Destiny, stop!" I heard Shay yell. I managed to drag Bianca to the car, but struggled to get her inside. Quickly, I looked around for Maurice, but it seemed he'd already pulled off. Bianca managed to get her purse from around her body and then sprint towards

Destiny. I noticed something in her hand, but couldn't put my finger on what it was. I ran after her, noticing both Shay and Destiny coming towards her.

"Fuck no! Hell nah!" I yelled. I reached Bianca and grabbed her and stretched my arm out to stop Shay and Destiny. "What y'all ain't about to do is jump this girl. I ain't letting that shit go down".

"Tell your bitch to watch her mothafuckin mouth" Destiny said. At this point, we were in the middle of the street. I noticed headlights approaching. Moments later, Maurice hopped out of his car.

"Man, what the fuck is y'all doing?" An eruption of yelling came from each girl trying to explain what was currently going on. I looked at Maurice, pleading with my eyes for help diffusing the situation. He grabbed Destiny and pulled her away while Shay followed behind.

"Weak ass bitch" Bianca said.

"Chill out bro".

"You just gon' let them talk to me like that?"

"Let them? I ain't letting them do nothing".

"You being a bitch just like them bitches. You don't never defend me about shit, but let one of them hoes say something".

"Call me another hoe or bitch and see what the fuck happens" Destiny yelled.

"Bitch wassup!?" Bianca yelled back, snatching out of my grasp and running up to Destiny.

"Destiny no!" I heard Shay yell. Before I knew it Bianca and Destiny were going blow for blow. I wanted to go break it up, but since it was one on one, I just said fuck it. Let them fight and get it over with. I was tired of all the arguing back and forth.

"Ahhh!" I heard someone scream. I looked and saw Maurice pulling Bianca away. "That bitch just pepper sprayed me in my fucking eye bro oh my God!!" Destiny screamed. *Pepper spray?*

"Bitch you got us fucked up!" Shay said charging towards Bianca. Bianca struggled slightly to get away. Just as she released herself from Maurice's grasp, Shay's fist connected with her fist. I ran over to break up the fight.

"Chill! Chill! Chill! It's over!" I yelled once I got ahold of Bianca.

"Weak ass bitches gon try to jump me?! Are you serious?" she yelled as I dragged her to the car. The girls exchanged obscene language, calling each other everything but the names they were given. Safe to say, tonight turned out to be a shit show.

I sat in the chair, getting my hair done. I was excited for tomorrow night. Raegan's family was throwing a Halloween party and me, Shani and Paris were going as the Mean Girls. I was going to look so cute in my little skirt and heels. The kids would be with their Dad, so I didn't have to worry about them. I lowkey wish Durrell would be there since I knew I would be drunk and horny, but it would be nice to have a girl's night. Just as I was dozing off, my phone vibrated. Looking at the screen, I saw that it was Destiny, Malcolm's cousin.

"Hey girl!" I answered.

"Autumn, you talked to your bitch ass baby daddy?" she asked sounding pissed the fuck off.

"Huh? No, I haven't talked to him today. What's wrong?"

"Me and his bitch fought last night and he let that weak ass hoe pepper spray me". I took the phone away from me and frowned. I was so confused.

"What do you mean y'all fought? What happened?"

"It all started because Shay asked Malcolm if he had heard from you and she got an attitude. She started talking about how you a hating bitter baby mama because when y'all met you had an attitude. Me and Shay like that doesn't sound like Autumn. Then she started saying how you went and told Malcolm she was weird and ugly and it went from there. Me and Shay decided we were leaving and I said she was a weird ass bitch, she heard me, asked me what I said and I repeated myself. It went from there. She ran up on me and when she realized she was losing she sprayed me with fucking pepper spray. My fucking eye still burning a little from that shit".

I was in shock. I knew that girl was weird, but I didn't know she was this weird. Plus, why am I even being brought up in their conversation? I mean, I get Shay asking about me, but that bitch Bianca needs to keep her mouth closed when it came to me. Also, why the hell is Malcolm just sitting back allowing that shit to happen? Your new girl arguing with your family? That ain't cool.

"Damn, I done lost respect for dog" I said referring to Malcolm. "I can't believe that shit happened. Are you ok?"

"Yeah, I'm good, but I wanna fight again" she said and I chuckled.

"Yo ass don't need to do shit else. Imma text you when I get done getting my hair done though". We hung up and I got back on Instagram thinking about the information that was just brought to my attention. After a few minutes of scrolling, I received a text message from Malcolm.

Kids Dad: Baby mama you got the kids costumes packed?

Me: Yeah. 3 tomorrow?

Kids Dad: Speak on what you know not what you heard stay out of shit that you don't know about Autumn

I was confused until I realized he had to see my IG post when I said "I lost all respect for dog". Chuckling, I rolled my eyes and texted back.

Me: Lol, boy go to hell

Kids Dad: You just be cool stop engaging in shit that got nothing to do with you

Me: Eat a dick

Kids Dad: Send a nigga. Can you do that? Stand on that when you drop them kids off tomorrow. Don't freeze up and act like you don't see nobody weird ass

*Me: *laughing emojis* this gotta be Bianca. Shut yo weak ass up weird bitch*

Kids Dad: I'm done going back and forth with y'all slow ass hoes send a nigga my way. Send somebody Autumn, please. Send yo nigga to me, I guarantee you that nigga will be missing some more fingers

After that, I blocked him. Now this nigga was acting weird to me just because his bitch got beat up? That's very crazy. I can say whatever the fuck I wanna say about whoever I want and can't nobody do shit about it. Now he wanna fight because I said I lost respect for him? Comical.

Once I was done with my hair, I took a couple of pictures and sent them to Durrell. Per usual, he loved and had a comment for every single picture, gassing me up. I loved the attention that he showered me with. I already loved myself, but he made me feel like I was the baddest bitch in the world and I appreciated that. Before I could respond to his texts, he called. Smiling, I answered the facetime.

"You aren't home yet?" he asked when the call connected.

"No, I'm on my way now" I responded. We made small talk until I remembered I had to catch him up about the latest bullshit with my baby daddy. Filling him I did my best to get his reaction while focusing on the road. Once at a red light, I came to a complete stop and looked at the screen. His dark chocolate face was twisted into a frown.

"What the fuck he mean bring a nigga?" he asked in a serious tone. I'd never heard this tone before, and I know I shouldn't be turned on, but I was.

"He can't fight me so he wants to fight a nigga. Specifically, you" I told him. Looking up, I saw the light had turned green, so I pulled off. Durrell chuckled.

"On God, bro don't want smoke with me for real. I'm not even about to entertain that shit. But if he threatens you again, it's definitely up there. That shit weak as hell. You mad because your bitch got beat up and you taking it out on your baby mama? How does that make sense?"

"I don't know, but he talking about have the same energy when I drop my kids off tomorrow". Again, he frowned.

"You want me to come with you?" he asked and I smiled.

"Nah, I'm not even gonna drop them off tomorrow. I don't know what they might have up their sleeves and I'm not about to engage in their bullshit, especially with my kids present. They've seen enough, especially MJ" I said suddenly feeling a wave of sadness wash over me. My baby had witnessed his parents going at it more than a few times and it wasn't fair to keep putting him in those situations. We continued to talk until I made it home and then disconnected.   The way Malcolm switched up shouldn't have surprised me, but it did a little. I don't know why I expected us to stay cordial, but whatever was about to come my way, I was going to handle it accordingly.

The next day, I woke up to hella DM's and missed calls from Bianca and Malcolm, threatening me and calling me out of my name. I screenshot everything as evidence just in case I ever needed it. There were two messages in particular that really stood out to me because it hurt. One message was from Malcolm saying that the kids were better suited with him because they were happier with him and I didn't take care of them the way that he felt they should be taken care of. The next was from Bianca saying that she's a better mother to my kids than I could ever be. Without a second thought, I dialed Malcolm's number.

"What the fuck do you want Autumn?"

"So now you want to try and take my kids away from me? Nigga, no judge will ever be stupid enough to give my kids to you!" Malcolm chuckled.

"Yeah, that's what you think. I ain't gon do too much talking, you might call the police. You know, because that's what you do, call the police because yo weak ass can't fight. It's alright though. Just make sure you drop my fucking kids off tonight and don't be a scary bitch when you do. And make sure they got enough clothes because they ain't coming back for a while" he said and then disconnected the line. I tried to call him back a couple of times but the phone went straight to voicemail. I sent a text.

Me: If you think I'm about to send my kids with you and that bitch after threatening to take them from me, you out your mothafuckin mind.

He didn't reply, but the message delivered so I know he'd see it sooner or later. That night, I dropped the kids off with Paris' Mom instead of Malcolm. He blew my phone up with even more threats, but I didn't care. Eventually, I just blocked him. There was no way in hell I was going to allow him and his girlfriend to disrespect and threaten me and then drop my kids off and expect for them to be treated correctly. Not that I really thought Malcolm would do anything to our kids, I know he loved them, but you can never be too careful. Especially with the way he's been acting lately. He was ready to fight and also wanted Bianca and I to fight, but for what? If I was being real, she deserved to get her ass beat, but somebody had to be the one thinking like an adult. Plus, what am I really fighting that girl for? Granted, she had a smart-ass mouth, but she can talk all she wanted. Her beef with me stemmed from her own insecurities about my opinion. That sounded like a personal problem to me.

Malcolm

"So, she really ain't bringing the kids?" Bianca asked.

"Do you see the kids here?" I snapped at her. I was pissed to say the least. I knew Autumn could be petty, but this was taking it too far. I never thought that she'd be the baby mama that kept my kids from me, but here we are.

"Don't fucking snap at me. I didn't do shit to you!" she yelled storming off.

Instead of arguing, I let her walk away. She was the reason I was in all this shit, and although I'd ride for my girl right or wrong, I didn't want to go without seeing my kids. Especially on Halloween knowing how MJ felt about going trick or treating. I never missed a Halloween or any holiday with them before so it made me a little sick to my stomach that I'd be missing this one.

I went into the kitchen and made myself a drink, tossing the liquor back, I embraced the burning sensation as it trickled down my throat and to my chest. I tossed a couple more shots back and then grabbed my phone off the couch in the living room. I attempted to send Autumn another text, but it wouldn't go through. After a few moments, the text bubble turned green, meaning that I was blocked.

"Are you gonna have an attitude or you gon come in the room with me?"

"Bianca, get the fuck out of my face bro, I ain't in the mood". She looked like she wanted to argue, but instead went back towards the bedroom.

Shit was fucked up all the way around. Ever since the fight between Bianca and Destiny, my family wasn't fucking with me at all. They all blamed me, saying that I let Bianca pepper spray Destiny and I didn't do anything to defend my family. I didn't even know Bianca had the pepper spray. I mean, I knew she had something in her hand, but I didn't know exactly what it was. I shouldn't even be surprised. My family blamed me for everything no matter what, and it wasn't a secret that they weren't really taking a liking to Bianca. My Pops expressed to me that Bianca's blunt personality was a little off-putting, but shit, my whole family had blunt personalities, they should be used to it. If it was anybody else's girl, it would be different, but because it's me it's a problem.

I'd always been the black sheep of the family and I know it's because I'm the only one who ever speaks up about how they really feel. Maurice wasn't going to say shit. He was always a laid back, go with the flow type of nigga, and then my sisters Shay and Parker were in a different league. They could do no wrong in my Pops eyes. The only one left was me. I thought I would always have Autumn on my side, but she picked a side making that post and acting the way she was. It was cool though, I had something for her ass. I guess I had to get used to it just being me and Bianca verses everybody.

Durrell

A few days had passed since Autumn told me about that bullshit with her baby daddy and it's been a few months since I'd been shot. I was almost back to me. I was able to move around freely, no bandages, no meds. My hand was still bandaged and the fate of remaining fingers was still up in the air, but other than that shit was back on track.

It was true when they said getting shot would do wonders for your career. My video on YouTube had almost 100,000 views and 20,000 likes. People were on me to get in the studio and drop my next song, and I was more than ready. Being cooped up in the house, I'd written a couple songs. One about getting shot of course, and then one about Autumn. I would never tell nobody about that shit though, not even Autumn. She didn't need to know she had me open like this. As if she could feel me thinking about her, I saw her contact picture appear on my screen.

"Wassup bae?"

"I'm giving you the green light to say and do whatever you wanna do to this bitch, I swear!" she yelled. I heard her sniffle, indicating she was crying.

"You crying? What the fuck happened?"

"This bitch keep fucking bothering me. Just last night he was calling me drunk telling me that he would never let anything happen to me, he misses his kids and he was sorry. Today, he wakes up talking about I'm a scary weak ass bitch and I don't know how to take care of my kids because every time they over there Armon has a rash or MJ is always hungry. Like I don't know how to take care of my kids! Then Malcolm talking about he's gonna take me to court for custody of them and I'm scary and don't wanna fight. I'm so tired of this bitch. He would never be able to take care of my kids the way I do and he knows that. I'm so fucking pissed Durrell" she cried. I felt bad for my baby. I've been through similar shit with my baby mama's so I knew this was all smoke and mirrors, but she didn't. However, Malcolm's threats didn't sit well with me. If he wanted smoke, he could get it fasho.

"Calm down baby, I'm on my way" I assured her. Not wasting any time, I made a phone call.

"What up bitch" Isaiah answered after the third ring.

"Where you at gang?" I asked not wasting any time.

"Crib. What's the deal?"

"I'm about to come scoop you. I'll explain in a minute" I said and hung up without further explanation.

I hopped in my car and sped to Isaiah's getting more irritated by the minute. It was one thing to go back and forth with your baby mama about the kids, but to be going back and forth with your baby mama about some shit that really has nothing to do with her is beyond me. Granted, I was on the outside looking in, but if it's one thing I know, it's Autumn, and her ass doesn't lie to me. I'd take her word over anybody's.

Pulling up to Isaiah's crib I honked the horn a few times to let him know I was outside. A few minutes later he was getting in the car.

"Wassup gang" he greeted.

"What's the deal".

"The fuck is wrong with you?" he asked. I took the opportunity to feel him in on what was going on between Autumn and her baby daddy. Isaiah and Autumn went way back. It's because of Isaiah that we even met, and I knew he loved her like a sister.

"What the fuck is wrong with that nigga? He ain't even cut like that" Isaiah said when I was done.

"Exactly, but shit, he keeps telling Autumn to bring a nigga, so here I come. Imma see what the fuck is up with him".

"You really about to pull down on this nigga after you just got shot?"

"Hell yeah. It's Autumn nigga. Plus, I know that nigga ain't really on shit" I told him. He shrugged. I knew even if he didn't really agree, he would ride with me right or wrong.

Pulling up to Autumn's, I hopped out and hurried to the front door, banging on it.

"The door was unlocked while you banging on it like the police" Paris said snatching the door open.

"Wassup cuz" I greeted. "Where she at?"

"I'm right here" Autumn said coming down the steps. She looked pissed off, but still beautiful. She had on a black sports bra with the matching leggings looking thicker than cold grits.

"Are you ok?"

"I'm okay, but I'm still pissed the fuck off. I'm tired of this bitch" she said frowning her face.

"Don't worry. Imma take care of it. Where's your phone?" she pointed to her phone on her desk. "Let me get that nigga's number". She wasted no time unlocking her phone and going to her contacts. I entered his number in my phone and called it.

"Hello?"

"Aye bro, I tried to stay out y'all shit, but you keep bringing my name up. Telling her to get her nigga like I ain't nowhere around. Here I am, so wassup? Drop the lo".

"Sayless" he said and disconnected the call. I waited a few minutes for the location to come to my phone, once it did, I looked at Autumn.

"What?" she asked.

"I'll be right back" I said kissing her cheek.

"Be careful" she called after me.

"Always baby".

We made it to the destination, and I looked around.

"I remember Autumn telling me he lived in an apartment complex".

"I don't give a fuck who crib it is" Isaiah said lifting up his shirt revealing his strap.

"Facts".

Going back to Malcolm's number, I tapped on it and held the phone to my ear. The line rang a couple of times before going to voicemail. I hung up, waited a little while and called back. This time, the phone went straight to voicemail.

"He ain't answering?"

"Hell nah, this nigga is a hoe" I said shaking my head. I knew he wasn't cut like that but to see him bitch up like this was a little shocking.

We waited around for about ten to fifteen minutes. I even went as far as taking a picture and texting this nigga to show him that I was at the location he sent, he never responded.

"Man, I ain't about to waste no more time on this bitch ass nigga" I said pulling off.

We made it back to Autumn's house just as she was finishing up working.

"What happened?" she asked.

"Your baby daddy is a hoe sis" Isaiah said sitting on the couch.

"Yeah, tell me something I don't know". Shaking her head, she looked at me waiting for me to fill her in. "Wow, are you serious?" she asked once I was done. I nodded my head to confirm. "I wonder what house that was because she lives in Canton and he lives in Southfield in an apartment complex". I shrugged my shoulders.

"I don't know, but I told you he wasn't cut like that. Nigga will do all that talking to you, but won't say or do shit to me. Weak as hell".

The four of us decided to grab food and watch a movie We all had a good time laughing and joking with each other.

"Bae, I'm about to take Zay home" I told Autumn standing up. She nodded her head.

"You coming back?" she asked looking up at me with those big eyes of hers.

"You such a brat" I chuckled. "Yes, I'm coming back girl. Right back". I said kissing her lips.

Autumn

"Bitch I'm a better Mother to your own kids than you could ever be. They might as well be mine". I'd never forget those words. Me and the girls had a great night at the party, but the next day, it was back to the bullshit. Bianca blowing up my phone from fake accounts, harrassing me. I've blocked so many pages, I couldn't keep up anymore. The last thing she said was that she was a better mother to my kids than I could ever be. That set me the fuck off. Finally, she'd gotten me out of my character. I wanted to pull up on her so bad, but Durrell, Paris and Shani stopped me, reminding me that if I go to her, she could easily call the police and I'd be in jail.

My baby daddy was showing his true colors and it hurt me for my kids more than anything because it didn't have to be like this. We hadn't said much to each other in the past few weeks. Thanksgiving came and went and now here it was almost Christmas and he's seen the kids maybe three times.

We'd initially agreed that we'd meet in a public place to ensure that no bullshit would go down in front of the kids, that way he could take them and spend time with them. That lasted for a week, and then he started insisting that I drop them off at his complex since I told him he couldn't come to my house. I refused to do that, reiterating the fact that I didn't trust him or her and I refused to act like a fucking fool in front of my children. Of course, he took it as me being scary, and hasn't bothered to ask for them in a while. I got MJ a cell phone so that he could communicate with his father and other family members so I know he at least talked to MJ every single day.

"Bro, don't cheat!" I hear MJ say. I looked up, and the sight before me caused me to smile. Armon, MJ and Durrell were all sitting on the edge of my bed with their eyes glued to the TV. Armon and Durrell were playing 2K against each other. They did this often and every time it got on my nerves. Of all the TVs in the house, they had to invade my space in my bedroom, but I loved it. I loved the bond that Durrell had with my kids and I loved that they loved him back.

In the weeks that had passed, I met a lot of Durrell's family and even met his kids, who also met my kids. They seemed to get along great, bonding over video games like any other boys. His daughter was a sweetheart but I could tell she had some sass to her, and I loved it. He'd even started consistently posting me on social media. Not that I asked him to, but it seemed like almost every picture I sent him, he had to show the world. I thought it was so cute. The boy was obsessed. I couldn't lie, I was too. He had my nose wide open.

We spent Thanksgiving at my Mom's before he went off to be with his family and I ventured off to be with my Dad's side of the family. We decided that Christmas morning he'd go and see his kids of course and then he'd come over here before going back with his family at his aunt's house. He asked if I wanted to come, but I declined. I knew Christmas was going to wear me out. I wouldn't want to do anything but lay in my bed and watch Christmas movies.

I scrolled through Facebook, laughing and sharing funny post. I noticed that I had a notification on messenger and went to it. I noticed that the notification wasn't in my regular inbox, so I went to the message requests where I found the message waiting.

Rochelle Harrington: Are you fucking Durrell?

*Rochelle Harrington: *missed audio call**

*Rochelle Harrington: *missed audio call**

Rochelle Harrington: Answer

I frowned. I glanced up at Durrell who was oblivious to what was about to go down. He looked so happy playing the game, he didn't even know that shit had just hit the fan.

Me: Yeah, I am. Why?

Rochelle Harrington: Lol. Y'all just fucking or that's your nigga?

Me: If you have to ask that question then you already know the answer, right?

Rochelle Harrington: He's definitely in a relationship with both of us sis, hate to break it to you

Me: Oh, really?

Rochelle Harrington: Absolutely. I saw you post about him when he got shot and I asked him about it but he said he wasn't fucking you.

Again, I glanced up at Durrell. My blood was boiling.

Rochelle Harrington: You bought him that Nike tech?

Me: Yup.

Rochelle Harrington: Yeah, I thought so. He told me his grandma bought it, but I knew that was a lie.

Rochelle Harrington: Well, you do what you want with him. I just wanted to let you know. And, I definitely fucked last night and this morning. But go ahead and have him. That man will never be faithful to a soul.

*Me: Lol nah I'm good. You can keep your baby daddy. I'm glad you told me now before I bought Christmas gifts. Good looking sis *laughing emoji**

*Rochelle Harrington: *laughing emoji**

I quickly took screenshots of the messages just in case she wanted to unsend anything and make it look like I'm talking to myself. I sat in silence, trying to gather my thoughts. I told this nigga time and time again; he didn't have to lie to me. My mind flashed to all the late-night conversations we've had, the parked car conversations, all the time spent. Then I started to think about the nights he wasn't here. It wasn't often, but I can think of times where I wouldn't see him for two or three days at a time. We'd talk, but we weren't in each other's face. I started to wonder if he was with her whenever he wasn't with me. Playing happy family over there.

Out of the corner of my eye, I watched as he took his phone out and read some messages. His body shifted slightly, and I knew that it had to be her texting him. He scrolled for a few moments before quickly tapping away on his screen and then shoving his phone in his pocket.

He started the game with MJ again and I noticed him turn his head to look at me out of the corner of his eye then quickly focus his attention on the game. He wasn't slick. *Yeah nigga, you've been caught.*

Durrell

Fuck. Fuck, fuck, fuck.

I definitely didn't want shit to come out like this. I didn't even know Rochelle knew who the fuck Autumn was. Well, I take that back. I knew. She'd asked me about Autumn right after I got shot. The question caught me off guard because why would she pick her out of all the females to react to that post? I told her that was my first and she asked if we were fucking. I could have told her the truth, but I wouldn't dare. Rochelle is a fire cracker. Any little thing will set her off, and I was trying to keep the peace for as long as I possibly could.

"I'm about to go to the store really quick. You want something?" I asked Autumn. I studied her face trying to gauge how she was feeling. If she was upset, she was doing a damn good job hiding it.

"Nah, I'm ok bae" she said and smiled.

Her smile was fake as hell, and if you didn't know her for real, you'd think she was fine. But I knew better. That smile didn't reach her eyes like it normally did. I walked over to her and kissed her cheek. I half expected her to move her face away from my lips, but she didn't. I was confused. I was used to getting cussed the fuck out. Hell, if I'm being honest, there's been more than a few times when Rochelle has attempted to beat my ass. Throwing anything she could find. This right here was new territory.

Walking out of the house I thought of all the possible outcomes. Really, this could go one of two ways; Autumn actually wasn't pissed and understood and nothing changed, or she was done with my ass.

"Fuck, all my shit is in there" I thought glancing up at her bedroom window. I had shoes, clothes, and my Xbox up there. "Damn I hope she don't fuck that shit up" I mumbled.

Pulling off, I made my way towards Rochelle's house. I knew exactly what to expect from her, so I wasn't really nervous. Honestly, I just wanted to get the argument over with. Rochelle stayed exactly eight minutes away from Autumn, so I made it there in no time. Using my key, I entered the house. As expected, Rochelle was in the living room waiting on me.

"You're a fucking liar. You really stood in my face and lied to me. I thought you was done with that shit!" Rochelle yelled getting straight to it.

"I ain't gotta explain shit to you Rochelle, you ain't my girl". A shock expression came over her face.

"Since when nigga? You wasn't saying that shit when your ass was just over here fucking sucking and eating up all my food. You weren't saying that when we were just out for my birthday or when you got shot!"

"Cut the shit. You were barely there when I got shot. Yeah, you came to the hospital and you looked out taking me to the doctor a couple of times but that's it".

"So that voids everything else that I've done for you? What do you want me to do drop everything to be at your beck and call? Like I don't have kids to raise and a household to maintain!?"

"Don't act like I don't help with that shit Chelle".

"Well, I let your bitch know everything and it seems like she ain't fucking with you my boy. You a dirty dick ass nigga. It all makes sense now. All of a sudden you started to get distant. You weren't spending half as much time as you used to over here, and then you started to come get the boys and take them with you instead of just staying here. Oh my God" she said as if a lightbulb clicked in her head. "You had that bitch around my fucking kids!?"

she screamed.

For a moment, I wanted to tell her the truth, but I didn't want to set her off more than I already had. More than that, I didn't want to hurt her feelings. Rochelle knew me very well. If I had someone else around my kids, she knew that meant I felt like that person was solid and would be around for the long haul. She knew that from first-hand experience.

"Nah man. There you go jumping to conclusions. She ain't been around our kids" I lied.

"You expect me to believe that? You've been out here lying about everything else but I'm supposed to believe that? How many times do we have to go through this shit bro? Bitch after bitch! Really, I wouldn't even be mad if it was some random bitch that you just started fucking, but your first? You really went all the way back to your first?! Like got damn". At this point, she was venting to herself. I don't even think she realized I was in the room anymore. "I can't do this with you anymore. You're going to have to make a decision right here and right now. No more back and forth between us. Pick a side. Are we going to try to make this shit work for real or do you want to be with her?" she asked.

My eyes went from the floor, to her face. Looking her in her eyes, I could tell that she was hurt and it fucked me up because it wasn't my intention to hurt anyone. Shit with Autumn and I happened so quickly, I didn't have any control over it. I didn't plan on falling for her. I didn't even plan on fucking her for real. I initially thought she was just going to be my dog, but here we are.

"You don't hear me talking to you?!" Rochelle yelled, throwing a shoe at me in the process. "Me or her!?"

I swallowed spit and blew out a deep breath that I didn't even realize I was holding in.

"Rochelle, you know I care about you and I love you. I wasn't trying to hurt you. I didn't even think it was a big deal since we aren't together and haven't been together. I apologize for leading you on and not being honest when you initially asked me".

"How long you been fucking with her?"

"Why does that matter?"

"How long?" she repeated.

"About six months" I admitted.

"Wow, and you still haven't answered my question so I guess that's my answer".

"Rochelle..." I started but she put her hand up, silencing me.

"I need to hear you say it. Who are you choosing? Her or me?" she asked folding her arms under her breasts.

"It's her".

"Get the fuck out!"

"How are you mad at me? I never got mad at you about none of these niggas you been fucking with on and off. I never questioned you about shit. I let you do your thing, but every time I do something I'm in the wrong. At least I told you!"

"You told me!? Nigga you lied straight to my face three months ago and you been fucking with this bitch for six fucking months?! Are you kidding me?!"

I blew out a frustrated breath. I wasn't going to win this argument.

"You're right, and I apologize, I really do, but let's not sit here and act like you're little miss innocent because you're not".

"Just get the fuck out Durrell. You made your decision" she said and walked away.

Walking back to my car I thought about what just took place. That actually went way better than I thought. I just knew she would tweak out. The fact that she didn't kind of bothered me, but I couldn't harp on it. What's done is done. Now, I had to worry about Autumn. She was calm as hell when I left her. No telling what state she was in now that she's had a little time to think about shit.

I made it back to Autumn's house in record time and just sat there collecting my thoughts. I officially ended things with Rochelle for her and I felt like I made the right decision. I know that my heart is with this girl and she's who I wanted to be with.

My phone vibrating on my lap caused me to snap out of my thoughts.

Sunshine: Are you coming back?

Me: Do you want me to come back?

Sunshine: Yes.

Me: Ok

Little did she know, I was already outside. Usually, I was good with words, but I'm struggling trying to find the words to say to this girl. Hell, what was she about to say or do to me? Never in my 28 years of living have I been this nervous about confronting my girl about my bullshit. Finally, I said fuck it, it was now or never.

Walking in the house, I noticed that it was quiet as hell, so I figured the kids were asleep. I didn't smell any bleach or hear any music, so maybe she wasn't that mad. I walked up the steps and opened the door to the bedroom. She was still in the same spot that I left her, on her phone. She looked up and immediately put her phone down when she realized it was me. I closed the door behind me and sat on the edge of the bed. At this moment, I was thankful for this big ass bed because I wasn't in her arm's reach.

"Are you going to be silent or are you going to talk?"

"What do you want me to say?"

"Something. You should have a lot to say".

"You thought I wasn't coming back?" I blurted out. She tilted her head and frowned slightly. I don't know why that was the first thing out of my mouth, but it was the first thought.

"Really? That's what you thinking about? That's what you have to say to me right now?"

"Sorry, it was the first thing that came to mind".

"So, talk".

"What do you want to know?"

"Everything. Start at why you felt like you had to lie to me after all the conversations that we've had? I asked you outright were you still fucking around with your baby mama. I asked was there any feelings there. I asked you! I told you I'd understand. Shit, I was still going to fuck with you because that's what I wanted to do. Like...damn" she paused.

"I usually always have something to say, but I'm at a loss for words right now. Thug ass nigga, and this 5 foot 2 inch girl got me nervous and loss for words" I said chuckling. She wasn't laughing though.

I looked up at her and the sight of her face crushed me. She looked so sad. Since we've been messing with each other, I've never seen her upset or sad outside of the situation with her baby daddy. To know that I hurt her feelings hurt me. It fucked me up to see Rochelle hurt as well, but this was different.

"I really put you on a pedestal. Why? I don't know. I guess because of all of our history. Even through all the bullshit we went through when we were kids, I never felt like you just flat out lied to me. I never felt like you didn't give a fuck about me until now. You didn't take my feelings, or shit, her feelings into consideration. You only thought about you. And it's really not the fact that you were still fucking with her. If you had been honest from jump when I told you I wanted to spin the block on you and been like 'aye, I still have a situation with my baby moms', I would've understood that and still fucked you because that's what I had my mind set on. But you didn't do that. If I would have known I would have guarded my heart. I wouldn't have caught feelings and now, it's too late. To make it even worse, I feel like I lost my friend and that's what hurts the most" her voice cracked.

She looked up and blinked a few times before looking down and putting her hands in her head. I watched as two tears dropped and hit her black comforter. That fucked me up. If it's one thing I hated, it was to see a female cry. Especially one that I gave a fuck about.

"Damn Autumn, don't cry. I don't even know what to say to you for real. I'm sorry man. I never meant to hurt you, I swear".

"I'm just disappointed in you I really am". She wiped her tears and looked at me with the saddest eyes.

In that moment, I didn't know what to say but the truth. I was very vulnerable with her and let her know exactly how I felt about the situation with Rochelle and our situation.

"I'm sorry. The last thing I wanted to was hurt you. I love you so much" I said scooting closer to her and grabbing her hand. Thankfully, she didn't pull away. We sat in silence, neither of us knowing what to say next. "Well, I guess I should go ahead and go" I said standing up and clearing my throat, not knowing what else to do.

"You're leaving?"

"You don't think that's best?"

"If you walk out of that door, I will never talk to you again so I think it's best for you to sit back down. Although my feelings are a little hurt and I'm disappointed in you, I'm not ready to walk away from you. I feel stupid for saying this, but please don't make me regret giving you a chance to redeem yourself". I could tell she was dead ass serious. I walked over to her side of the bed and sat directly in front of her. I leaned towards her and kissed her forehead.

"I promise, I ain't gon hurt you again. She gave me an ultimatum, and I chose you. I'm gonna choose you every single time.

Since everything went down last week, Durrell had been stuck to me like glue, and I can't say that I was complaining. The entire situation was fucked up, and yes, my feelings were hurt, but I believed he deserved a second chance. I went into the situation with rose colored glasses in a way, but I vowed to make sure my eyes were wide open now.

Durrell and I were around the house cleaning up and preparing for our game night. It was supposed to be a Christmas theme, but only the girls were participating because the guys were lame. We were all going to wear our Christmas pajamas and have a good time. I was ready to get fucked up with my people and I hoped his friends and mine got along. It shouldn't be any issues though.

ding I heard my phone alert me of a notification. Walking over to my dresser, I grabbed the phone and looked at the screen. I sucked my teeth when I saw who the notification was from.

Rochelle Harrington: He better not have you around my kids or Imma beat yo ass

Rochelle Harrington: Y'all can do wtf you want but if he has you around my kids Imma beat yo ass and his, he knows that. Don't let him get you in no shit sis

Instead of feeding into the bullshit, I locked my phone and continued to clean up. Little did she know I've already been around her kids. They've even spent the night at my house a couple of times. I could understand where the hostility was coming from, but I just didn't have it in me to entertain it because once I start, there's no stopping, so I try to keep my other side locked away for as long as I possibly can.

***

Game night went very well to say the least. We all had a great time. Durrell and I were so fucked up that we couldn't even get out the bed the next day. Thankfully, my mom had the kids so I didn't have to worry about them.

"I'm never drinking with yo ass again, I swear".

"You had the time of your life, stop it". We were currently in the bed. I was hungry and wanted to get food, but I just didn't have the strength. I was in so much pain, I wanted to cry.

"Bae this shit hurt".

"I'm starting to feel better for real. Try to get some rest. Imma go get you some pain pills and a Vernors" he said and I nodded my head.

I must have dozed off and didn't realize it, because when I opened my eyes, the room was completely dark. I sat up and realized it was night time and my bedroom door was closed. I felt a little better, but still, I needed to put something on my stomach and take something for the pain. Opening my bedroom door, I heard Durrell downstairs on the phone.

"Do what you gotta do then Rochelle, I don't give a fuck. That won't change shit" he said in an angry but hushed tone. I stood by the steps so that I could hear a little better. "Yeah...alright" he said and then it grew silent. I took that as my cue to make my presence known and started down the steps. When he noticed me, he smiled.

"How are you feeling?"

"A little better. I feel like I need to eat". He shook his head, turned around and dug in a black grocery bag that sat on the kitchen counter. He pulled out a Vernor's, a stand back and some plain lays chips. I smiled. He knew that was my go-to whenever I wasn't feeling the best.

"Thank you" I told him.

"So, when are we wrapping the kids' gifts?" he asked. Christmas was next week and although I'd already purchased everyone's gifts, I hadn't wrapped a thing.

"We? You don't even know how to wrap gifts".

"You gon' teach me" he said matter-of-factly. I chuckled.

"I barely know how to do the shit myself, I can't teach you".

"Ok Imma just watch".

"Whatever".

"Aye, look at these videos from last night" he said unlocking his phone. He showed me four of five videos of us from last night. I burst into a fit of laughter watching us act a fool.

"I don't remember any of that. Send that to me".

After a few hours, I Was feeling better and decided to go ahead and get my kids. Durrell told me he had to run to the studio, which was fine. Since the day he got caught he started sharing his location with me to try to put my mind at ease, but that really didn't do anything because I had no idea where his baby mama stayed. He could still be over there and I wouldn't know. Still, I tried to trust him and put those thoughts to the back of my mind.

***

My favorite holiday was here. Christmas and my birthday were really top tier for me. I loved watching my kids faces as they opened their gifts, and I also loved when everything was about me. MJ made sure to wake me up early so that they could go downstairs and open their gifts. It was a little bittersweet for me this year because Malcolm wasn't here. I'd gotten so used to it being the two of us on Christmas, so the fact that it was just me right now made me a litle sad. I knew it was for the best though.

After the kids open their gifts, I made them something to

eat and then got them ready for the day. They were going with their dad for a few days. In the midst of me getting the kids together, Durrell came over.

"Alright, where's my onesie?" he asked. I giggled. I can't believe I actually got him to agree to this. I hurriedly went up to my room and gave him the onesie that matched mine. "Where's the boys'?"

"They didn't want to wear it anymore so I let them take it off" I shrugged. He put his onesie on and stared at his self in the mirror. I laughed uncontrollably. He looked so cute.

"Lowkey, I look better than I thought I would in this" he said feeling his self.

"Period bae" I continued to laugh.

"Come here, with your phone" he said. I got off the bed and stood in front of him in the full-length mirror. "Take some pics. We look good" he said and I smiled. Doing as he said, I snapped countless pictures and then showed them to him.

"Yeah send me all of those" he said slapping my ass. "You sure you don't want to go with me to my auntie's house? I don't want you to be here by yourself".

"Yeah, I'll be fine. I'm gonna enjoy the peace and quiet and chill".

"Don't be over here in your feelings man" he said.

"I'm not!" I said playfully flipping him off. He could always tell when my vibe was off, even if it was just slightly. It was a gift and a curse.

I dropped the kids off and made it back home in record time. Stripping out of my clothes, I climbed in the bed and made myself comfortable. In the middle of watching a movie, I got this feeling in the pit of my stomach. Without so much as a second thought, I grabbed my phone and checked Durrell's location. It said that he was eight minutes away. I remember him telling me that his aunt lived close as hell to me and that he'd be back once the party was over. Ignoring the feeling that was still at the bottom of my stomach, I continued to enjoy my me time.

The next day, I woke up alone. I wasn't really tripping though. I figured he'd gotten too drunk to drive like he always did and I'd talk to him later. I checked his location again and it was still in the same spot as last night. I sent him a quick good morning text and then got myself together. Paris was over to hang out with me, so we were about to go get the kids and come back and watch Christmas movies. Initially, the kids were supposed to be gone for two more days, but Malcolm insisted that something came up and he needed me to come get them. I didn't care, I missed my babies anyway.

"I'm about to ride past where this location takes me" I told Paris as I pulled away from my house.

"Why?" she asked confused.

"I don't know, I just have a feeling". That same feeling that I felt last night had returned, and I couldn't push it down.

"Well, you know I'm with whatever, let's go". I followed the GPS and drove to the destination. I noticed Durrell's car as soon as we turned the corner onto the street. Getting closer, I looked at the house as if it could provide me with answers to the questions I was forming in my head.

"Hmm, well he's definitely here" I said pulling off.

Pushing my thoughts to the back of my mind, I went and grabbed my kids and then went to grab smoothies and something to eat. While in line my phone started ringing, but it was the messenger tone. I frowned. Nobody ever called me off messenger. Looking at the screen on my car, my stomach got tight. *Rochelle Harrington.* I looked back at the kids and then at Paris who was already looking at me. Instead of answering, I ignored it, not wanting to engage in any of her antics in front of my boys. She called right back and I ignored it again. My phone dinged again alerting me that I had a message. I wasted no time looking at it.

Rochelle Harrington: Yeah bitch you knew where he was lol

"He's gonna break up with me" I blurted out.

"Girl, what? Why would he?"

"I don't know. I'm trippin".

"Yeah, you think he's gonna leave you just because that bitch called?" she asked, but I ignored her. I was too busy in my own thoughts. Once we got home, I got the kids settled and just as we were about to turn on a movie, Durrell texted me. The first thing that I noticed in the thread was that he stopped sharing his location. I frowned.

Bae: Good morning Autumn, we need to talk. Are you at home?

Me: Ok

Instead of us having our movie night, I just wanted to lay down. I felt like I wanted to throw up and cry. My intuition never ever lies, so for me to have this feeling so strongly, I knew for sure I was about to lose my man today.

I woke up from my nap and saw a man's silhouette. Completely opening my eyes, I saw that it was Durrell walking back and forth in the room. I rubbed my eyes trying to wake up and figure out what was going on. I sat up and looked around the room. I noticed a trash bag in front of the dresser. I looked back at Durrell and noticed him unplugging his game. He grabbed the cords from behind the TV and then placed the game and controller in the bag. He clearly didn't notice that I was awake, because he grabbed the bag, exited the room and went down the steps.

I thought he left for a few minutes but then I heard the side door open and close. Next, I heard his heavy footsteps approaching and finally, his face appeared in the hallway. When he noticed that I was awake, he paused for a split second and then continued to walk towards me.

"Hey" I said lowly.

"Hey". The energy in the room was weird between us. I couldn't pick up on his mood which was weird because I could always tell how he was feeling.

"Why are you taking your stuff?" I asked getting off of the bed. He let out a deep breath and then looked at me.

"Look, Autumn, we've been cool for a really long-time and..." he said but I cut him off.

"We've been cool? Really? Spit it out Durrell. Just tell me what you have to say" I said not wanting to hear a long-drawn-out speech.

"I can't be with you Autumn".

TO BE CONTINUED...